SCOTT BARRY

HUNTING EVERETT REDDING

SHORT STORIES

Published in the United States by:
Happy Living Books Independent Publishers
www.happyliving.com/books

ISBN: 978-1-7321152-0-0

Written by Scott Barry
Edited by Jonathan Grant

For permission requests, please contact:
hello@happyliving.com

Printed in the United States of America

Disclaimer

CONTENTS

BIG DAVE

Looking back, it was the little things that finally drove Dave to the point of not caring—or in his case, killing his daughter. At least that's what he always complained about when he sat behind the thick plexiglass divider, phone pressed to his ear. The little things. It wasn't like I hadn't heard most of them before. He always started off complaining, pounding his fist on the counter, cheeks burning red, same stoned-faced guard standing behind him and saying, "For the hundredth time, calm the fuck down."

Dave hated authority.

Then again, who couldn't relate to the frustration of a broken tooth on a plastic fork, a faulty zipper on a new coat, an impossible-to-open corn chip bag, dropping the fresh Popsicle that's only passed out once a week, catching

1

a fingernail on a sleeve, even the lack of privacy in a six-by-ten cell, especially when taking a shit? Dave even reached into the past and complained about his wife's thin-lipped mouth and cold thighs, his car refusing to start on a cold winter morning and slow drivers. And when he finally arrived at school just as the bell rang, late as usual, Dave couldn't help himself from wading into the annoying chatter of his third-grade class like an angry drill sergeant. "Line the hell up!" And when he finally got home, hoping to unwind and have a cocktail, he was met with the constant wailing and begging for attention of his two-year-old daughter. "Kid came outta the womb bawling," he complained.

It became common knowledge that at some point that year Dave began yelling at his class beyond the typical barking about lining up or raising hands. That year, Dave crossed the line, taking it much further, and darker, making derogatory comments about his students' smarts and looks—and even their families. More than one parent complained. His deep, angry voice echoed into my classroom and down the hall to the point that I ordered Teddy, the goofy kid who sat near the door, to close it whenever Dave went off. It got so bad that other teachers complained and gossiped about him, mostly to me, because they knew we were friends and I taught fourth grade. Some even complained to Principal Ramirez. One day in the teachers' lounge over an English muffin and black coffee she whispered to me, "What's got into Dave?"

"Nothing I know of," I said, half-truth, part lie. Sure, any one of Dave's complaints were annoying enough on their own, but none of them, even all of them combined, should have led to any of this shit.

Big Dave

"But what about the gun?" I said to him through the plexiglass on one of my first visits to Mule Creek State Prison. "What the hell were you doing with a loaded gun on your desk?"

"So, I like messing around with guns," he said. "That against the law?"

"You were drunk."

"So, I like messing around with guns when I drink," he said, staring at my soul with empty blue eyes. "That a crime too?"

*

A while back, Dave told me the story he told detectives: that it was all an accident. That his daughter had been playing in his home office, full of energy, running around, out of control, climbed on his desk, stumbled and fell out the open window. But I knew things about Dave no one else knew until the trial. Nothing too serious, unless you're not a teacher and expect only "teacher things" to happen at school—and not real-life things like Dave bending the P.E. teacher over his desk and fucking her with the door locked. The rumor mill said she was gay, but Dave found out she was at least bi. And the best fuck he'd ever had. When he first told me out on the playground during recess, I told him I didn't want to know any of it, but then couldn't help myself from muttering, "*That* good, huh?"

"World class." Dave grinned. "Woman has muscles in her toes."

3

"In her toes?"

"I'm just saying," Dave said with a wink before hollering at one of the kids. "Hey, Jason, keep your dirty hands to yourself!"

Maybe that's why I kept making the hour drive up into the foothills to visit him in prison even after my wife and in-laws and everyone in town told me I was crazy to do so. Maybe I kept going because I thought he'd confess it all to me. Maybe I thought I was his priest. But Dave clung to his story, even when I couldn't be subpoenaed to testify against him because he'd already been tried and convicted. Even when I swore to him that I'd never tell a soul, Dave stuck to his story.

But what *was* the truth?

Like everybody in our tiny farming town, I had been surprised, even shocked to learn during the trial that Dave had been long collecting Nazi memorabilia. A swastika flag, an engraved SS Luger, a vintage boot dagger, some war medals and even a first edition *Mein Kampf.*

"What the hell?" I said when I read it in the paper. Sure, Dave had a big, square Arian face with a bald head, pale blue eyes, and skin so transparent you could see thick blue veins on just about all six-foot-six of him. But if you saw him in the teacher's lounge with his khakis and running shoes and button-down dress shirts, you would've trusted him with your kid, any kid, without a thought. He was an effective teacher too. A real disciplinarian. His classes posted some of the highest test scores in the state. He'd been honored a dozen times by one group or another and was once a finalist for National Teacher of the Year.

"Hey, man, wasn't like I was hurtin' anybody, just

collecting stuff," he shot back when I asked during a later visit.

"But *Nazi* stuff?" I asked.

"People collect all kinds of goddamn things. Doesn't make 'em murderers."

"That's not what I'm saying."

"Sure sounds like it," he said, and tugged on the lapel of his orange jumpsuit. "And what about you? Getting blowjobs from that fat bus driver. You're lucky her fatter husband didn't hunt you down and give you something to think about."

Yep, that was Big Dave. He knew right where to go and didn't mind going there. He even seemed to enjoy it. His mind was cunning like that, sharp to the point of sadistic. Long before that night, he'd told me over beers that he hated his wife. "Dumb bitch," he muttered into his drink, "just the sight of her makes me wanna puke. Some nights I lie in bed next to her and imagine she's dead."

"How does she die?" I asked, wishing I hadn't. Dave's eyes narrowed, and he got this weird, glazed look like he was thinking about killing *me*. So I said, "I mean, how do you *hypothetically* see her dying?" I couldn't believe I said that either so I downed my beer and looked at the bartender. "'Nother round." I could feel Dave staring at the side of my head.

"Strangled, drowned, pushed off a cliff," he said. "Just as long as she leaves me the fuck alone."

"Why don't you divorce her?"

"Why don't you divorce *your* wife?"

There's Dave again. Knowing right where to go.

*

At the trial, Dave's wife discovered he'd been fucking the PE teacher for over a year and had even promised to marry her—once he got rid of his wife. At least that's what the PE teacher said under oath, though she never said how he might do it.

But that's not what bothered the lead detective with the '70s mustache about Dave. It was his intelligence. That and the distance of his daughter's body from their house. The detective kept coming around asking questions weeks after she died from "falling" out of their second story window.

"Hey, man," I said to Dave the day after seeing the detective leave. "You oughta get yourself an attorney. Who knows what he's thinking?"

"I didn't do anything; it was an accident. What the hell do I need an attorney for?"

"You never know."

Dave was too smart to be a third-grade teacher. He should have been a brain surgeon or an astrophysicist. He was that smart. And he always had a good answer for every question the detective asked. Too good.

"I'm innocent and that detective's a fucking clown with a stupid mustache," Dave complained.

Either way, his little girl had fallen too far away from the house. She was only two. None of it made sense to anybody—except Dave.

During the trial the prosecutors dissected the differences between falling and being thrown. They argued that a two-year-old couldn't jump that far if she tried. They painstakingly recreated their theories, each scenario ignited by the explosion of a father's drunken rage and the strength of a man Dave's size. First, the backhand swat from his desk with one of his thick paws, then the forehand swat, like swinging a tennis racket; then the throwing possibility, underhanded, like throwing a bag of trash out the window. After all, she only weighed thirty-five pounds. According to the prosecutors she landed in the driveway about as far as a grown man could throw thirty-five pounds, accounting for momentum lost breaking the screen.

The screen, that was a problem for everyone, including me.

Thing was, none of us could picture a two-year-old girl jumping out of a second story window in the first place, especially through a screen, or falling by accident and landing that far from the house onto a concrete driveway. (Why was the window even open in the middle of winter?)

Nobody except Dave.

And that wasn't the only problem with his story. Why was his daughter playing on his desk? A desk with a bottle of vodka and a loaded .357 revolver sitting in plain view and within her reach? Dave didn't deny he'd been drinking that night. The emergency room attendants all swore on the stand that Dave smelled of booze. Did alcohol impair his judgement? Ignite his rage? Even his wife couldn't deny that he'd been drinking and ranting that night—and now a little girl, his little girl, *her* little girl, was dead.

*

I looked down the row of cubicles at the other

visitors. Everybody seemed happy. But why? Hadn't their lives been ruined by some evil force? Wasn't that force sitting across from them? Or had they forgotten the horrible deeds and the pain and the heartache—and moved on?

Dave looked the same as he always did: as if he were about to say something but not saying it. Like there were a thousand thoughts in his head but none he could put to words.

My mouth moved to fill the silence. "So, you still plan on heading out of state when you get out?"

"Hell, yes," he said. "Anything but this socialist state. California's gone straight to shit." Dave had been convicted of voluntary manslaughter and child endangerment, two strikes but only seven years. The case was circumstantial at best and detectives couldn't prove that his daughter's death was premeditated, and they didn't try. Seven years for killing his daughter. Another strike, felony drunk driving or something, and he'd spend the rest of his life in jail. "Fuck that, we're going to Idaho, Montana, Wyoming."

"We?" I said.

"The wife, dude, she's sticking with me."

"She is?" I said, my voice tinged with high-pitched doubt. Dave's chin tilted toward his chest and his eyes grew dark. He looked at me as if I were a conspirator, even though last month when I came to visit, Dave told me his wife had filed for divorce. "Fuck her," he had said, pounding his fist on the counter.

"I thought you guys were done."

"Naw, she gets it, man. She's almost forty. She knows she won't find anyone better than me."

That's when I wondered which was worse: a man killing his daughter or a wife staying with the man who killed *her* daughter? How could she forgive Dave? Forgive him for throwing their two-year-old daughter out the window?

"She knows I'm no murderer," Dave said, looking at me on the other side of the plastic, his eyes wide. He looked at the guard then back at me. "Just like you do."

Just like *I* do? What the hell did I know to be true? I knew what Dave had told me. I knew what he had been accused of. I knew what he'd been convicted of. And still, it all seemed unthinkable—that the hands of the man sitting across from me, the hands of a teacher, a father, a friend, killed his own daughter.

"Time's up," said the guard as he walked over. I took a breath, shifting in my seat. God only knows what stories these plexiglass dividers could tell.

"You comin' by next month?" asked Dave.

"I'll do my best."

"I didn't kill my little girl," he said, same as he did every time I left. "Sure as hell wanted to kill my wife, but I didn't kill my little girl."

"I know, Dave. See you next month."

WHERE I'M FROM WE CALL 'EM PIT BULLS

Sunday night I walk into the living room to tell Lana I'm moving out. Before I can get a word in, she closes her book and says, "Let's get a dog."

"We're not allowed to have 'em in the building," I say.

"Landlord won't notice."

"Won't notice a *dog*?"

"He's too old," she says.

"Too old to notice a dog?"

"Too old to care about a dog."

"How old," I ask, "is too old to care about a dog in a building that *doesn't allow dogs*?"

"*Old.*"

I sigh and walk to the fridge and crack open a beer and take a sip.

"You're just closed-minded from growing up in that backwards ass cow-town!" she hollers from the living room.

"And you're damn pushy from growing up in this hornet's nest!"

I'm from a place called Walnut Grove, population 725. Lana's from a place called Los Angeles, population shit-fuck.

*

Monday, when I get home from substitute teaching, a color print of a terrier with floppy ears and his head tilted perfectly for a Hallmark card is on my desk. I should've never bought her that color printer for Christmas. Sent my credit card over the max. And now it's helping her campaign to get a dog in our apartment *that doesn't allow dogs*—plus we both know it's long past time for me to leave. We also both know it's why she wants a dog.

After dinner I'm watching reruns of SportsCenter wondering how I'm going to tell her it's over. Us. She plops down on the couch next to me and flips open her laptop. She says, "You can look-up dogs online now."

"Huh?"

"South Central Animal Shelter. They have a lot of cuties."

"Where I'm from we call 'em pounds." I change the channel to Antiques Roadshow. "Bet it's a bunch of agro Pit Bulls with clipped ears and their balls still hanging."

Where I'm From We Call 'Em Pit Bulls

"American Staffordshires."

"Where I'm from we call 'em Pit Bulls."

Lana gives me the eye. She turns her computer toward me. She scrolls through a surprisingly handsome lineup of canines on the South Central Animal Shelter's website. Walked myself right into that trap.

"I don't know about having a dog in the city," I tell her. "Looks like a lot of work. Walking them on a leash every day, taking them out to piss and shit at all hours. And I'm not psyched about picking up dog shit with a plastic bag. In Walnut Grove we use a shovel and toss that shit in the ditch."

She puts a hand on my knee and makes her best puppy dog face. "But this is something we could do together."

"I don't know. I just don't know."

"What the hell don't you know?" she asks, eyes wide now.

I mute the TV. "There was this time I was driving through Beverly Hills feeling like a peasant, you know, in my old truck. No hubcaps. Faded paint. I pull up to a stop sign and right next to me is one of those Rolls Royce Phantoms or whatever the hell they're called idling at the curb. The driver looks at me over the top of his designer sunglasses like I've come to mow his lawn. Some cheesy Dean Martin looking guy. Then I notice his passenger door is open and when I turn the corner, I see a tiny purse-dog the size of a large rat, hunched over, pooping in the grass of the parking strip. And the dog's owner, some middle-aged woman with a spray tan and a botoxed face, *is holding a plastic bag in her palm under the little dog's ass*. Can you believe it? Shitting into its owner's palm. And the rat-dog was wearing an evil little smirk like *it* was the master. Made me feel better about my truck, but it just seemed wrong."

"What's your *truck* got to do with anything?"

"Where I'm from we take our dogs out hunting in the back of our trucks and they sleep in a pen and do what they're told."

"Then don't let *our* dog poop in your hand . . . or in your truck."

This is why I don't talk to her. I always lose. I sigh and turn the TV back on. I want to turn to her and say, "I'm leaving." But I don't have the nerve.

*

The next morning, Tuesday, lying in bed, she asks me to meet her after school at South Central Animal Shelter to look at dogs. She knows it's on my way home from Plasencia Elementary in Echo Park, out in East Los Angeles, where I've been subbing in the same autistic class for months. Most subs won't teach special ed. They say it's too stressful, but for me it somehow works.

"Take the 10 to the 405," she says with a breathless laugh after our first sweaty time under the covers in months. She's devious, a real pro, and a hell of a lot smarter than me. She graduated with honors from NYU. I barely graduated from Sacramento State. I'm a tenant in her world and she knows it.

Toward the end of the day she calls me at school on my cell phone to remind me about the shelter, but I can barely hear her because ten-year-old Byron is having a tantrum. I hold out the phone so she can hear for herself. "Jesus, that's loud," she says. "Is he okay?"

"He'll be fine. But my head's throbbing."

"*Please*."

"I don't know," I say and hang up.

*

Walking the kids to their bus I imagine the South Central Animal Shelter flea-ridden and covered with dog shit. I imagine the 10 and the 405 inching along in a noxious haze of exhaust. I tell myself there's no way in fucking hell I'm driving an hour through that mess to get assaulted by fleas and shit.

When the last of my kids boards the bus, I walk back to class determined to call her and tell her there's absolutely no way I'm going to look at flea-fucked-shit-ridden *pound* dogs. But when I arrive at the gate, the security guard, a gray-haired Hispanic man who's never spoken a single word to me, holds out a tin and asks, "Altoid?"

"Why not?"

I suddenly remember Lana's sweet smile and our sweaty time under the covers.

*

When I pull into the second-floor parking lot at South Central Animal Shelter, Lana is waiting for me, all smiles. I've never seen her this happy. What a smile she has. What a face. What a beautiful woman. Especially when she's happy.

15

We walk downstairs to the waiting room and sit in plastic chairs. The shelter is surprisingly clean and sterile and smells more like a hospital than a dog pound.

"*Shelter*," she corrects me and smiles, somehow reading my mind. How does she do that?

A round African-American woman with a somber expression opens the electronic metal door with the push of a button. "This way."

We follow her into a corridor lined left and right with kennels full of dogs. Two, three, four to a kennel barking away. I stop to look at an old bulldog, huffing and slobbering as if he's on his last breath. Maybe he is. I look at Lana who's two steps ahead of me and already locked in a staring contest with a female black Lab mixed with something or other. I know that look on Lana's face. I walk over and have a look at the pooch.

"I don't know," I say.

"You don't know what?"

"She's too small for a purebred Lab, especially with that random white spot on her chest."

"So she's mixed."

"I don't know."

Purebred black Labs are the only dogs my family has ever owned. Born and bred to hunt. And this mutt is so small it would look silly riding in the back of my truck, especially in Walnut Grove.

Lana asks to see the black dog.

"Which one?" the woman asks, straining to hear over the barking and whining of caged dogs, especially the grandad rottweiler, head back, howling at the top of his lungs. A Pitbull with clipped ears, just like I predicted, barks

16

low like a predator from the back of the kennel.

"The little black one," Lana says.

"With the sad eyes," I add, surprising myself.

Lana looks at me: *He noticed her eyes and how sad she must be locked up in dog prison. He has a heart after all.*

"Can't see that dog, yet," the woman says. "Just came in this morning. Come back in a day or so and I'll pull her out for you."

Lana frowns.

"What're the dates on the kennels for?" I ask, noticing each cage has a date in the near future written on it.

The woman looks at a date next to a list of random numbers, like serial numbers, then at her watch. It's a few minutes after four. "We keep 'em a minimum of seventy-two hours. Then, day of the date, if a dog isn't adopted, we usually put 'em down the next morning."

I look closer at the date on the next kennel over. A scrawny mutt with the curious eyes of a collie and the athletic body of a pointer stares back at me.

"Put 'em down?" I ask.

"Euthanize them."

"Tomorrow?"

"Some of 'em tomorrow. Maybe that one."

I look at the mutt. He looks back at me with eyes of innocence. He's already dead and doesn't know it. I turn for Lana, hoping she didn't hear the word "euthanize" but she's already at the metal door having heard it all. She looks at me with a long face. She's never had a dog before or seen one die. I have. Our first family dog, Shane, died of distemper. Mack got run over by a truck. And Buddy died on the vet's table after his stomach burst.

17

Scott Barry

I've seen plenty of dogs die. That's how it is in Walnut Grove—where I'm from.

By the time we get home, Lana's given the little black Lab a name. Sadie. Sadie with sad eyes and a little white spot on her chest.

"You shouldn't have named her," I say. "You just shouldn't have." Then I try not to think of Sadie and those sad, pleading eyes, begging to be taken home and kept warm and safe.

To clear my mind, I walk down the street to Starbucks and search online for apartments you can afford as a broke writer day-jobbing as a substitute teacher. It's definitely time for me to leave.

That night Lana searches through her massive CD collection and finds the Beatles tune, "Sexy Sadie" and plays it over and over, dancing around our apartment in her underwear. She's wild. I've never seen her this happy.

"Sexy Sadie, how did you know /
The world was waiting just for you"

Lana finds Sadie's photo on the South Central website and prints a color picture and sets it on my desk.

Hi Dad, she writes on the photo.

I walk from my desk to the fridge and grab a beer and turn on the Lakers game. They're playing the Sacramento Kings. Shaq throws one down over Webber on a lob from Kobe. The crowd roars. I groan.

I wish Lana would listen to me. I wish I wasn't such a coward. I wish I could tell her what we both already know.

Where I'm From We Call 'Em Pit Bulls

*

By fifth period on Wednesday my head's about to explode from all the screaming and tantrums. Samuel keeps taunting Byron, "Suuuucker!" Byron keeps stamping his feet and crying, "Samuel said to me . . . " Jason runs out of class and me after him. Bobby rolls a poop out of the bottom of his jeans that I have to dispose of with a paper towel in the toilet. And Best, the only girl in class, spends the entire day trying to pronounce my name, "Mr. Luuunnnsforrrd." I want to go home and lie down and ice my skull. My cell rings. It's Lana. I answer. "So?" she asks.

"I can't go today. Just can't."

"But what if someone adopts Sadie?"

"You shouldn't have given her a name yet. You just shouldn't have."

"Whatever." She hangs up. My head is pounding so hard it feels as if my brain is thumping against my temples.

When I get home there's another picture of Sadie on my desk. And the note: *I would love for you to be my dad, Sadie.*

What the hell am I supposed to say to that? Especially when Lana pulls the covers over our heads that night and jumps on me with that look in her eye. I've never seen her like this. She's gone wild. This is great. And confusing.

*

She calls me three times Thursday morning. I can't answer my cell phone because I'm missing my teaching

19

assistant and my head hurts. I don't know if it's an official migraine, but it feels like a hatchet buried in my skull. Then again, who doesn't have migraines working in Room 25 at Plasencia Elementary, the autistic room tucked way back in the far corner of campus?

When I get home the photo of Sadie is gone. After eating dinner in silence, Lana drops her dishes in the sink and says, "Please." She starts to cry. I want to tell her I've found a studio apartment in Koreatown and could be out in a few weeks—but don't because she's already in a state over Sadie and doesn't handle bad news well.

She's still crying that night when she crawls on top of me and presses her warm naked body into mine tighter than she ever has.

*

Lana is still at work at *Yoga Works* out in Santa Monica when I get home from school on Friday after another fucked-up week. I have a beer and sit on the couch and stare at the ceiling and think about Sadie. She doesn't have to be my dog. I don't need to take her to Walnut Grove and let her ride in the back of my truck. She'll be Lana's dog and ride in her Volkswagen Golf. Besides, she's just a dog. A sad little dog. A *city* dog.

I pop open another beer, take a sip, and dial the number for South Central Animal Shelter. A woman answers. "I'd like to know if Sadie is still available," I say.

"Sadie?" she asks.

"Oh, right, hang on." I search my desk for that photo of Sadie. Where the hell'd I put it? It had a number on it, like a serial number, like the numbers on the cages. Finally, like the genius I am, I look in the trash. Aha! I uncrumple the photo and read the number aloud as if I'm reading a winning lotto ticket.

"Hold please," the woman says. Muzak plays on my phone. I look around our apartment and imagine Sadie lying in her little doggie bed that we'll get for her from the Petco on La Brea. Eating out of her little bowl in the kitchen. Playing with a squeaky chew-toy at my feet. Sexy Sadie with the sad, sad eyes. And happy me, playing under the covers with my city girlfriend—morning, noon, and night.

I take a sip of beer and run a hand through my hair. Man, what a week. I love those kids but they're killing me. The Muzak cuts out.

"Hello?" the woman from the shelter says.

"Right here." I'd almost forgotten I was still on hold.

"That dog was euthanized at 10:45 this morning."

I set my beer on the coffee table and take a deep breath.

"Hello?" the woman asks.

I exhale loudly. "Euthanized?"

"Put to sleep." I look at the spot where Sadie would have slept in her bed, where she would've chewed toys at my feet. "You still there?"

"Yeah," I say and hang up the phone.

What now? What's a man supposed to do knowing Sadie's sad eyes will follow him for the rest of his life? How does he tell his woman that her Sadie is dead? Sexy Sadie with the sad, sad eyes. Dead because he "didn't know." Didn't know if he wanted to have a dog in the city. Didn't know how to tell her that all their fighting and ignoring each other had finally burned a hole of resentment in his heart. Didn't know how to tell her goodbye.

I call back the woman at the shelter.

"I thought you weren't supposed to put 'em down until the day *after* the date on their kennel," I say, my voice raised. "That's *tomorrow*."

"Normally we do, but she'd been here seventy-two hours and we can only keep the dogs that people are the most interested in, that we think have the best chance of getting adopted. Especially before the weekend when most people come through. We have limited space."

"Nobody asked about her except us?"

"I'm sorry, sir."

"No, ma'am, I'm sorry."

What the fuck? How could Sadie stand there with those sad eyes, alone, nobody stopping to pet her, hold her, rub her little nose—for the last few days of her life?

*

When I wake up, I'm lying on the couch, face buried in my arm, drool stain on the cushion by my mouth.

In the bathroom I splash water on my face. It's dark out. What time is it? What the hell happened? Why are my eyes so red? Then I remember hanging up the phone and falling into the couch and crying, then sobbing, then heaving, then hyperventilating, then pounding on the couch with my fists. *What the fuck?! She had another day! She's only a dog! A pound dog! That I didn't even know! How was I supposed to know that no one would want her? Stop fucking looking at me with those sad eyes! Stop!*

Where I'm From We Call 'Em Pit Bulls

I sit on the couch and stare at the phone. I don't remember crying that hard when my best friend died. What the fuck? There's no good way to say this. There just isn't. No lie has ever existed in the history of mankind capable of hiding the truth about something like this.

I pick up the phone two, three, maybe four times before deciding to wait until Lana comes home. Yes, that would be much better. To have her within reach so I can hold her and wipe *her* tears. Then again, maybe it would be better to tell her now, give her a chance on her long commute home from Santa Monica to process her sadness and anger and resentment before taking it all out on me—or punching me in the side of the head like she did that one time.

The phone rings. Lana's calling from work. I answer it without thinking. I immediately regret it.

"Forgot to take my meds today," she says. I know her blue days, Sadie or not. Sure, they're fewer now with her new meds but they still come from time to time. "I checked online about Sadie," she says.

I swallow hard, my heart lowering into my stomach. "You did?"

"Yeah, she's gone."

I suck air into my lungs, ready to speak, ready to apologize, ready to defend myself. I killed Sadie. Not with a car or a gun—but with indecisiveness, with laziness, with procrastination. It had always been regular life shit, like not renewing my driver's license on time or forgetting to pay a parking ticket—or retreating into myself and sabotaging every relationship I'd ever known. But now it was Sadie's life. And the time has come to confess. God help me. "I'm—"

Scott Barry

"Someone must have adopted her," Lana says.
"Adopted her?"
"I hope she went to a nice home."
I hear a bark from the sidewalk.
"I'm sure she did." I walk to the window.
"Maybe it wasn't meant to be."
"Yeah, maybe it wasn't."

GAYLA KNOWS

Gayla had been practicing all morning for the deposition and, if someone pinned her down, she would have admitted to practicing for it ever since she was subpoenaed a month ago. "Big companies always settle," her husband told her as she smoked a cigarette out the kitchen window. "There ain't gonna be no damn trial."

"But what if there is?" she asked and took a quick puff.

Gayla was sure there'd be a trial, that she'd be called to testify in front of the judge, the jury, the whole town. She'd been there, after all. She tried to save Susan Gardner from herself.

"Either way, just tell the damn truth," her husband said.

Easy for him, what'd he need to remember besides putting his boots on the right feet and feeding his dog when he got home from work? Sure, he'd done a year at Sacramento City College before quitting to work full-time at his uncle's fertilizer plant, but that didn't exactly make him Einstein. "Some city slicker lawyer in a three-piece suit's gonna strut in there like a peacock and ask you a bunch of stupid questions. Just look him in the eye and tell 'im the damn truth."

Gayla sighed. Her husband hated the city, and he never wore a suit, even to a funeral, so what did he know about suits and lawyers aside from what he watched on TV? And just because nobody in the city could teach him to hunt or fish or mix aqua ammonia in the big mixer down at his uncle's fertilizer the plant, that didn't make them morons.

"If you say so," Gayla said, stubbing out her cigarette.

*

Gayla looked at the directions in her hand with one eye, doing her best to keep her other on the road. Her writing was smudged. She looked at the side of her hand blotted with ink. She was sweating even though it was a cold winter morning and she hadn't bothered to turn on the car heater. "*Get off at J Street & turn rt... first building on rt... park in underground garage, elevator to 11th floor, Suite 1114.*" But she didn't need the directions anyway. She'd memorized them the minute the woman from the law office said them over the phone.

If Gayla was known for anything, it was her memory.

It drove her friends and husband nuts. "Memory like an elephant," he'd say. "Woman oughta be workin' for the CIA."

Gayla pulled into the parking garage, found a spot near the elevator and sat for a moment. She couldn't remember the last time she was this nervous. Only thing that came to mind was the last game of Bingo at last year's Catholic bazaar for the big screen TV, but that seemed silly now.

Gayla climbed out of her truck and locked the door. She walked to the garage elevator, pushed the up arrow, and thought about parking garages and elevators and Sacramento and how much she disliked cities. And Sacramento wasn't much of a city, but it was the state capitol because of the Gold Rush all those years back and had enough tall buildings to have its own professional basketball team. The only reason Gayla ever dragged herself to Sacramento was to buy in bulk at Costco or shop at Macy's for clothes. She'd owned a Macy's card her whole life like her mother had before she died of cancer. But the thought of traffic and stoplights and one-way streets and everybody in such a hurry gave her a headache. Back home in Four Corners they didn't have a single stoplight and never would if she had anything to say about it.

*

Gayla stepped off the elevator, turned left, walked down the red-carpeted hallway and arrived at Suite 1114. Not a soul. Or a sound. The building felt deserted. There wasn't even a name on the door, just the number. She remembered the name of the law firm: Smith, Lee, Bertrand & McGann. She expected to see a receptionist or some fake flowers like a doctor's office, not a silent door. Does a person knock on a door with just a number? Was this the janitor's closet? Did she have the wrong number? She double-checked the paper in her hand. She knocked and waited. She tilted her chin down and looked at her watch, 10 a.m. on the nose. "City people, they're always late." She felt small knowing that she could be anywhere on time because, maybe, she didn't have enough to do. "Guess that makes me stupid."

Gayla was quick to go to stupid. That's what most people thought about her growing up. Even with her great memory, she didn't manage school very well. Nobody could figure it out. She just hated sitting in class all day listening to boring teachers drone on about dead presidents or the anatomy of a frog. But she passed the GED her junior year without studying and then, while working check-out at the Big Store in Four Corners, discovered she was good with numbers.

Gayla could do most figures in her head. Tough ones even. Some customers would wait in her line to ask her to do some sums for a laugh. When she'd pull up their total on the till and it matched what she'd predicted, they'd cackle and elbow each other and nearly fall out of the store.

Fun as it was, after seeing *Rain Man,* she stopped with the numbers bit because she started wondering if she could be autistic. She'd always thought her head was too big for her body and her eyes might be too close together and she did like to knit and rock for hours in her chair, and, well, that's a helluva thing to think about yourself so she quit the

Gayla Knows

Big Store and went to work for a local cherry packing company. Before she knew it, she was back doing numbers, this time working the weigh station where the fruit trucks came and went.

*

Gayla stomped on her cigarette. "The hell with it." She closed the exit door she'd found at the end of the hall and propped open with her foot, and marched up to Suite 1114. She turned the knob and went in. Not much of a suite or a room. The only furniture was a long wooden table surrounded by leather chairs and a single window. Gayla walked to the window. From the eleventh floor she could see for miles, to where the rows of stucco houses and strip malls ended, all the way to where the fields began.

"Gayla?" asked a voice behind her. She spun, startled. A suited-man with a handsome face and slicked-back hair approached her, offering his hand. "Nelson Lee, attorney for the Gardner family. Sorry I'm late." She stared at him, trying to catch her breath. She noticed the yellow legal pad under his arm. She shook his hand, a hand too soft for the hand of a man.

"Gayla Johnson, nice to meet you."

"Sorry, if I startled you," Nelson said.

"That's okay, it was so quiet and then—"

"Would you like some coffee, a bottle of water?"

"No, I'm fine. I stopped at Alma's on the . . . the little coffee shop in—"

"Four Corners?" he said.

"Right, Four Corners. You've been there I guess."

29

"I had lunch at Alma's the other day. Friendly little place."

"We like to think so."

"Please . . . have a seat." Nelson motioned to a chair.

"Is this where we're going to have the . . . do the deposition?" Gayla asked, sitting. Nelson looked at her a moment, longer than you ought to look at someone while you're thinking.

"No, we'll be upstairs in our main office."

"This isn't your office?"

"It's *part* of our office," Nelson said and sat at the end of the conference table. The head of the table. The spot where her husband always sat at the dinner table. "Don't worry, the deposition doesn't start until eleven."

"But your secretary said ten."

"I was hoping we'd get acquainted before everybody else showed up."

"Who else is coming?" Gayla asked, already feeling like someone had lied to her.

"Besides us," Nelson said, "there'll be a lawyer for Universal and a videographer for documentation."

Gayla pulled a tissue from her purse and wiped her nose. "You're gonna be taping it?"

She hated having her picture taken, let alone being filmed. She didn't like her smile and knew she had a double chin. She'd also read in *People* that video cameras make you look fat. Plus, she hadn't had her hair done in over two weeks on account of her regular gal at the beauty shop winning the Hawaiian vacation in the 4-H raffle.

"In case a jury needs to compare it to your testimony in court."

"To see if I lied?"

Nelson reclined in his chair. "It's just a formality."

"Is there gonna be a trial? My husband said Universal would probably settle. He says they have insurance for these kinds of things, and it costs more to go to trial."

"Sometimes," Nelson said, flipping a page in the yellow notebook, then another, and another.

"Think they'll settle this time?" Gayla asked, eyeing the handwritten notes on the flipping yellow pages.

"Depends on how we do today . . ." Gayla waited for Nelson to finish the thought, but he didn't. "So, the family tells me that you and your husband are farmers."

Now, right there, damnit, right off the bat she knew she couldn't trust him. Not a chance in hell Susan's family told him they were farmers so why say that?

"Well, not really, I mean, sure, we own sixty-acres or so that my husband inherited from his father. It's not much of a farm, open ground mostly, a few cherry trees, nothin' you could live off."

"But it's a farm."

"We let someone else do the farming. It's not much, couple thousand dollars a year." Where Gayla came from people listened to what you said and went on to the next thing or left it alone. But Nelson's smile cut off her thinking before his voice did. This was exactly why she didn't like cities or people who lived in them.

"You know, Gayla, where I come from, you're a farmer whether you own a thousand acres of corn or one acre and an apple tree."

"I guess . . . to city folk."

"Exactly. City folk on a jury. Who trust farmers."

"I wouldn't trust all of 'em."

"What I mean is, people in the city tend to trust salt of the earth folks, honest and hardworking. And we want the jury to trust you." He adjusted his legal pad and shifted his legs. "So, today, if I say you're a farmer, you are. Okay?"

Gayla clicked her fingernails like she did when she got nervous playing Bingo, which usually led to cuticle cuts. "Okay, if you say so," she said and looked out the window. She wanted to run and hide like a little girl and pretend none of this had ever happened. Damn that fat, sweaty man from Universal Rent-A-Car. If he'd listened to Gayla, Susan would still be alive. If Gayla had stayed, Susan would still be alive. If only she had stayed.

Nelson put his elbows on the table and interlaced his fingers. "I'm not trying to put words in your mouth, Gayla, but if the jury doesn't trust you, we'll lose."

"Okay, then we're farmers, I guess."

"It's better that we don't *guess* about anything, Gayla. And don't be afraid to be direct and firm. Make eye contact when you're answering a question. If you look down or away or even at me, they'll think you're lying, even if you aren't. Keep a straight, honest face."

Goddammit, if Nelson wasn't *telling* her what to do and *say*. Blood came from her cuticles now. She pulled a tissue from her purse and nodded, hating herself.

"Okay."

Nelson took a loud, deep breath. "Now, the morning of Susan's death you went to her house."

Gayla wondered whether it was best to say, *yeah, yes, right,* or *correct*.

"Gayla?"

"Yes."

"Why?"

"Because Chip called and—"

"Mr. Gardner?"

"Yes, Susan's husband."

"Good. We need to speak very clearly; we need to assume the jury doesn't know who or what we're talking about. That way we leave no room for their lawyers to manipulate you, to make you out to be . . . " he paused, " . . . less than truthful."

"Okay, then," Gayla said. "Susan's husband Chip called me and asked me to check on her. He said she was having a bad morning."

"A *bad* morning?"

"She'd been drinking."

"And what day of the week was this?"

"It was a . . . a Wednesday."

"Now, Gayla, don't be afraid to speak firmly, like you know what you're talking about. Hesitation makes people wonder. What day of the week was it?"

"Wednesday," said Gayla firmly, her stomach churning.

"At approximately what time?"

"Late morning. Eleven. Eleven-thirty."

"Eleven-thirty. Good. And why did Mr. Gardner—Chip—ask you to check on Susan?"

"Well, since we lived right down the road he would call from time to time and ask me to check on her when she was having a bad day. You know, see how the kids were and all."

"Did this happen often?"

"Often?"

"More than once a week?"

"Sometimes. She drank a lot, but I guess you know that."

"*I* know it, but *you* need to say it—out loud. Get it clear in your head."

"She had a drinking problem. Chip worried about her and the kids when he was at work."

"Did you worry about her?"

"Of course, I did, I—"

"Why?"

"She wasn't well. Worse right before—"

"In what way?"

"She was depressed. Taking a bunch of meds, pills, God knows what. And she'd already gone away at least once that I—"

"Gone away?"

"To rehab or whatever . . . "

"A rehabilitation facility?"

"I guess."

Nelson tilted his head down and squinted his eyes at Gayla.

"I mean," said Gayla hesitantly. "Yes."

"Voluntarily?"

"*Voluntarily*? I don't know exactly, I mean—"

"But Susan did *agree* to go. It's not like they came and put her in a straitjacket and hauled her off in the middle of the night," Nelson said, suppressing a chuckle.

Gayla didn't think any of this was funny. And she wasn't one to laugh at someone else's problems. Especially someone who was dead and had three kids and was a kind-hearted person. "Of course not," she said.

"Then Susan went *voluntarily*. Sounds like it may have even been her idea."

"Honestly, I don't know, I don't think she really liked it there." Gayla stared at Mr. Nelson Lee, attorney at law, with his slicked-back hair and gold watch. "And I don't see what this has to do with anything," she said.

"As far as I'm concerned it doesn't," said Nelson. "Unfortunately—"

"I mean, are people going to know all this about her? She was a good person, it'll seem like—"

"Gayla, this is still just you and me talking. Nothing's on the record yet. But you can be sure Universal wants it to look like, '*Hey, if some suicidal nutcase wants to kill themselves bad enough in one of our cars, how can* we *stop 'em?'*"

"Is that what they think?"

"They'll be looking for anyway to make Susan appear responsible. An alcoholic. A negligent mother. Institutionalized. Suicidal. Imagine what a jury would think."

"But what do I say when they—I mean, everyone knows she tried a couple of times to—"

"That's why we're taking the time to make sure you don't injure the memory of your dear friend, Susan," Nelson said. "And sleep better knowing you didn't. She had a drinking problem. She voluntarily went into a hospital to get better—those are important words to remember, Gayla. Not an institution, but a *hospital* and *voluntarily*. It didn't work. It doesn't always. But she tried. That she also tried to kill herself doesn't really matter."

"It doesn't?"

"Who hasn't?"

"Who hasn't what?"

"Thought about it from time to time."

"Suicide?"

"Harming themselves."

"I haven't," said Gayla.

"C'mon, Gayla, everybody has at one time or another," Nelson said. "It's only human."

Gayla's eyes drifted to the dark wood table. Maybe oak. Definitely oak. "I'm sorry . . . I'm confused. What?"

"Gayla, stay with me on this. Because if you don't, we'll lose. Simple as that."

"I'm trying."

"And you're doing fine. Now, Mr. Gardner took Susan's car away?"

"Yes."

"Why?" Nelson said.

"Because he was afraid she'd hurt herself or the kids." *Why is he asking me questions he damn well knows the answers to?*

"How would she hurt them?"

"By driving when she'd been drinking."

"Chip was afraid she'd get into an accident?" asked Nelson.

"Yes."

"An *accident*."

"I don't understand."

"Susan would never do something like this *intentionally*," Nelson said. "People rarely kill themselves with cars and car accidents. The potential pain. The possibility they might survive."

But Gayla knew damn well what Susan was capable of doing to herself, but never to her kids. She fought off tears. "I don't know—I just don't want, you know, to let the family down. But at the same time, I don't want—I mean, I was raised to always—I know it'll sound corny but—I mean, her oldest, Kevin, he's almost fourteen. He wants to go to college." A tear escaped and she wiped it away.

Nelson leaned forward. He put his hand on Gayla's arm, but she couldn't feel it, couldn't feel a thing.

"Gayla, you're doing fine. Nobody's asking you to lie. But remember, Universal doesn't care about Susan, or her kids, or you. They care about renting cars and making money. 'Accidents happen,' they'll say."

"I guess so. Yeah."

"Now, that Wednesday, the day of the accident, you went to check on Susan."

"Yes."

"How was she doing?"

"Like I said, 'bad.' She'd been drinking all morning."

"How could you tell?"

"The sound of her voice. She was upstairs yelling at Kevin, the oldest. I stayed downstairs with the two girls. They were crying and then the doorbell rang."

"And you answered it?"

"Yes, I went to the door and it was that heavy-set"— she wanted to say 'fat and greasy'—"man with a brown clipboard and a white shirt with the Universal Rent-A-Car logo. He said he was 'delivering a car to a Mrs. Susan Gardner' and if I was her."

"And what did you tell him?" said Nelson.

"I told him I wasn't," said Gayla. "And that I was sorry, but he'd have to take the car back because Susan can't drive right now."

"That's exactly what you said?"

"Maybe not exactly, but—"

"We need to decide exactly what you said, Gayla. *Exactly.* He asked if you were Mrs. Susan Gardner and you said . . . ?"

"No, I'm not."

"And . . . ?"

"And I'm sorry . . . but you're going to have to take the car back . . . she isn't supposed to be driving . . . "

Nelson looked Gayla square in the eye. "She's been drinking. Do not rent her a car."

"What?" Gayla said, leaning back.

"I assume you would have continued with, 'She's been drinking. Do not rent her a car.'"

Gayla looked down at the floor for a moment. She was beginning to forget what happened that Wednesday morning. But how? She had been there at Susan's house. She knew what happened.

"'She'd been drinking. Do not rent her a car.' That's what you said, correct?" asked Nelson.

"I don't know, I—"

"Then *try* saying it. It might help remind you of what you said."

Gayla felt a pain. In her cuticles. And inside.

"Go ahead, give it a try."

Gayla took a breath. "She's . . . been drinking. Do not . . . rent . . . her . . . a car." She was certain she was going to vomit.

"Say it again," Nelson said, his voice deepening.

"What?"

"Say it again," he said.

"She's been drinking. Do not rent her a car."

"Good. And you were adamant with him, weren't you?"

"Well, I believe I just spoke in a normal tone of—"

"And you repeated yourself several times."

"What I said?"

"In a situation like that you must have repeated it."

"Honestly, I don't remember exactly. I—"

"During conversation we repeat ourselves all the time."

"I guess we do. I've never really thought about it. Honestly, I—"

"See, right there. You just did it, Gayla."

"I did?"

"Yes, you repeated several times: 'She's been drinking, do not rent her a car!'"

"I don't . . . I'm not sure I said that exact—"

"But you said something like it."

"I suppose I could have. I—"

"Then why not make it that? Sometimes we instinctually do things we don't realize. I wouldn't be surprised if you repeated yourself several times. Very adamantly. I wouldn't be surprised if you raised your voice."

"I don't know," said Gayla. "It's possible, I suppose."

"We can't *suppose* anything, Gayla. If we do, the family loses, Susan loses, the kids lose. You don't want that, do you?"

"Of course not."

Nelson stood from his chair and walked to the window. "You repeated yourself so many times and so adamantly that the man from Universal would've had to of been *deaf* not to hear you."

"I don't know now; I could have but—"

Nelson stared out the window. "But what?"

Gayla looked away. "Nothing," she said.

"Good." Nelson paced along the table. "Now, you said you could tell Susan had been drinking because of her voice."

"Yes."

"How else?"

"Her face and nose were red, like they got sometimes."

"And this happened when?" Nelson asked.

"After the man from Universal left. Susan came downstairs."

"Did she have a drink in her hand?"

"Yes."

"Did you see her take a drink?"

"No, well, yes, kind of. Susan didn't like to let you see her drink or show you what was in her cup."

"But she did have a cup in her hand."

"Yes."

"And what was in that cup?"

"Wine."

"Red?"

"Yes."

"And how do you know that?" Nelson said, sat, and

looked at his yellow legal pad.

"Well, like I said, her face, and I could smell it on her breath. She had one of those big plastic cups that she always carried around and said was iced tea."

"Did you actually see the wine in her glass?"

"No, I didn't—I never really—"

"But you knew it was wine."

"Yes."

"You could smell it on her breath."

"Yes," Gayla said.

"So, you didn't need to see the wine to know what it was," Nelson said. "You could see it in your mind, couldn't you?"

"Excuse me?" Gayla said.

"What color was the glass?"

"Blue."

"Think back, Gayla. That morning, in your mind you made a mental picture of red wine inside a blue plastic glass, didn't you?"

"I don't know, I suppose so . . . "

"And that picture, the one you have in your mind right now, is as real today as it was then because *there was red wine* in that glass, wasn't there?"

"Yes, there was," Gayla said.

"Then you saw it. Just like you see it right now," Nelson said.

"Okay, but I didn't really—"

"And that's exactly what you tell them. They'll ask, 'Did you actually see the wine in her glass?' And you'll say, yes, because you did." Gayla tried to breathe but couldn't get any air. She put her hand over her mouth. She could taste the acid of vomit in the back of her throat. It was bitter, like someone had just cum in her mouth. "Do you need a break?" Nelson said.

"No, I'm fine. Are we . . . are we going to start soon?"

"One last thing, Gayla."

"Okay."

"When you left Susan's house that day," Nelson said, "you did so reluctantly, didn't you?"

"Well, yes. Susan was in such bad shape. Maybe the worst I'd seen. Chip, Mr. Gardner, wanted a divorce. He told Susan that morning. I didn't know what to do. I didn't want to leave the kids there with her, but I had to go to work. I felt terrible—"

"Gayla, we all have lives to live. You couldn't have spent your whole day there, could you?"

"No."

"So, you left. And when you did, Susan was clearly drunk. She reeked of alcohol. Red wine to be exact. Heck, you could smell it from ten feet away."

"I could."

"Anybody could."

"I would think so, but—"

"And she was slurring her words, making no sense, behaving erratically—"

"Well, honestly, I don't—"

"Stumbling around. Drunk. *Obviously drunk*. To a child or a stranger."

"Honestly, she was bad, but I don't remember her being—"

"Gayla, listen to me—"

"I mean, what am I supposed to do? What's my

husband going to say about my testimony? He told me to—"

"Gayla—"

"I'm sorry, I can't just make things up. I have to live with this. You don't. You don't know what it's like in our town."

"Gayla—"

"People talk. I live there. See everybody every day. At the store. The post office. Alma's."

"Gayla—"

"I have to drive by that house every day." Gayla grabbed her purse and stood. "What if I had stayed?"

"Gayla, listen—"

"I mean, who's going to be at the trial? People I know? From our town?" Gayla made for the door. "I mean, I love those kids. But I don't know. I don't—"

"*Gayla, listen to me*," Nelson said. She stopped at the door, trembling. Blood from her cuticle had soaked through the tissue. She steadied herself with a hand on the doorknob and began to cry.

Nelson rose. "There's only one person who can stop this case from going to trial and that's you. Because this is what's going to happen today: Universal's fancy corporate attorney is going to try and get you to say that Susan Gardner wasn't just an alcoholic, which she was, but a functioning alcoholic who could maintain herself so well that nobody but those closest to her could tell she'd been drinking—and sometimes even they couldn't. He's going to try and get you to say that she was a bad mother, mentally unstable, and had been institutionalized on several occasions—against her will. On one occasion, by the way, she tried to hang herself with a sheet, and was so deeply distraught over her husbands' decision to divorce her and the likelihood that she would lose custody of her kids that she was on a suicide mission. A suicide mission not even her closest friends—you—or her family could stop. 'Not our problem,' Universal will say. 'We can't be responsible for the judgment of our drivers. What someone does with one of our cars once they leave our lot is completely out of our control. If someone wants to kill themselves bad enough, we can't stop them. We simply rent cars.' That's what they'll want the jury to think."

Nelson took a step toward Gayla. Her crying slowed. "But you told that man not to rent Susan Gardner that car. You were very clear. Adamantly clear. She was drunk. Clearly drunk, as you will testify. And still, he returned after you left—who knows what story she gave him and who cares—and drove her to the bank to get cash. And at the bank she made an ugly scene, by all eyewitness accounts and the video recording, and then he drove her to Universal's office—her trusty blue glass *still* in her hand—where they proceeded to do the very thing you told them not to: *rent her that car. And she paid with cash*. They even called her insurance company because she had no proof of insurance on her. They even sold her—*for twenty-five dollars*—a life insurance policy that was, of all things, and according to the fine print, void if she'd been drinking. Universal Rent-a-Car went so far out of their way to rent Susan Gardner that car, that some might call it great service. I call it gross negligence. Because your dear friend Susan took that car that they negligently rented her and wrapped it around an oak tree at eighty miles an hour and drowned in her own blood. And they're not responsible? They're not liable? What about Susan's kids? Who's responsible for them?"

Gayla leaned against the door. Nelson put his hand on her shoulder. "It's up to you, Gayla. You want justice to be served and Susan's kids financially taken care of? Then convince Universal's arrogant attorney that his client knowingly and negligently rented a car to someone who was obviously and plainly intoxicated, drunk, and that going to trial would be a mistake, *a costly fucking mistake*. It's that simple. Can you do that, Gayla?"

Gayla's lips trembled but no words came out.

"Gayla?"

She cleared her throat. "Yes . . . I think so . . . "

"You *think* so?"

Gayla thought a moment: "I can."

"Then do me a favor." Nelson turned Gayla by the shoulders to face him. "Nod when you say it." Gayla held her breath.

"What?"

"When you attach a physical movement to a thought, you implant that thought into your body via your brain. It becomes not only *your* truth . . . but *the* truth. That way, when you're sitting in front of the camera today, you can be sure your conscience and your heart are in the same place."

Gayla exhaled. "Okay." Nelson stared at her again without blinking. He was clearly waiting for something.

"What?" Gayla asked.

"You need to nod."

"Now?"

"Yes, now. Practice makes perfect." Gayla thought about home, and her husband, and Susan. She nodded. And hated herself for it.

"Good," Nelson said and checked his watch. "I'm

gonna get some coffee before we head upstairs. Would you like a cup?" Gayla thought about the bitterness of coffee. What she needed was a drink. Whiskey.

"Sure," she said. Nelson smiled his plastic attorney smile, rose, and walked to the door.

"And Gayla, if someone happens to ask you what we discussed today, your husband, for example, the best thing to say is that 'we were just getting to know each other.' Which I feel like we have." He smiled again. "Cream? Sugar?"

"Black, thank you."

"Black it is." Nelson opened the door and was gone.

Gayla walked to the window. Clouds had gathered but she could still see the patches of green and brown in the distance. Row crops and open ground. At least that's what they called them back in Four Corners. She looked at her hands. The blood had dried on her cuticles but her hands were shaking.

She clasped them to make it stop.

HUNTING EVERETT REDDING

I'm dove hunting with my best friend and hunting partner, Everett Redding. Where I come from a hunting partner is a life thing. I can't guarantee 100 percent Everett would call me *his* best friend or *his* hunting partner—it always seemed like Everett was his own best friend. Either way, I don't have any friends better than Everett so that makes him best.

*

It's the first of September. 1978. On the first of September we hunt doves, no matter what day of the week that is. School day, weekend day, Labor Day. Other months it's pheasants or ducks or deer.

47

Scott Barry

*

We're sitting at the edge of a freshly harvested safflower field. I'm crouched with my back against a telephone pole surrounded by a patch of Johnson Grass, its tall green blades providing nice cover. Everett sits down the line of poles next to the ditch. We're hunting the *afternoon flight,* the second of two daily flights. The first begins at sunrise when flocks of doves leave the tall oaks near the sloughs, where they roost overnight, to come to the fields to feed. Their favorite fields are freshly harvested safflower. I asked Dad once, "Wonder which came first, the safflower harvest or the opening of dove season?"

Like always, Dad looked off at nothing and took a drag on his Marlboro Red cigarette. "Don't know. Just how it's always been."

Once the doves have flown to the fields, they fill their craws with safflower seeds left behind by the harvesters. Then, with proud and puffy chests, they fly back to the oak groves for their midday nap, maybe stopping in a slough or canal along the way for a sip of water—or maybe, like Dad says, a stopover in a farmer's open field to nibble on bits of gravel to help digest their haul. Later in the afternoon—the second flight of the day—they return, just like we do, to the fields to eat.

We come to hunt. Everett and me and Dad.

I'm sixteen and Everett's seventeen *and a half*—but we're in the same class. Not that Everett was dumb. He only got held back in grammar school, landing in my class, because he was bored stiff by books and hated sitting on his restless butt all day. Our second-grade teacher, Miss

48

O'Connor, would slap him on the knuckles with her yardstick and bark at him to sit still, then look at me and say, "And you mind your own p's and q's."

*

I hear a single gunshot down Everett's way, echoing low and hollow.

Usually, it's two or three in succession, crackling sharp into the sky. Doves like to fly in packs and pairs—some say they mate for life—and they're damn hard to hit. People around here always say, "Doves fly too damn fast, can barely get your gun up and track them suckers." But I like that they fly fast, and when they see you, they dive and swerve like fighter pilots dodging enemy fire.

I stand to watch Everett walk out to pick up his dead dove, hold it up in triumph, like he always does, and smile my way. But he doesn't appear. A rare miss for him. Good to know Everett Redding's human like the rest of us.

About a hundred yards down the pole-line in the opposite direction of Everett, Dad sits on his wooden fruit box. I can see him clearly. Dad. He doesn't hide. He likes to sit out in the open, plucking doves from the sky with his 12-gauge pump.

I see his gun go up, sun glinting off its barrel followed by three successive shots.

Two doves drop from the sky. Both stone-dead though the second takes two shots. Coffee, Dad's black lab, retrieves the birds. Two quick round trips and he's sitting next to Dad anxiously waiting for the next bird to fall. Coffee's a good dog with a great nose.

Dad never budges the slightest from his box. Most people don't like to shoot sitting down because they can't swing their bodies, but he doesn't care.

Sometimes, for a challenge, he even shoots with one arm. "If he's any kinda shot, guy oughta be able to kill a dove with one arm," he'll say.

I look Everett's way. Still can't see him. Definitely missed that bird. And Everett likes to crouch low in the cover of the Johnson Grass that grows along the edge of the ditches, where its roots can get to water but where the farmer and his chopper can't get to the grass outta fear of fallin' into the ditch. Chopper and farmer. It's been known to happen.

A pair of doves fly right over Everett's spot and land in the safflower field. Not a sound from his shotgun. Everett must've been looking the other way. Doves sneak up on the best of us but rarely on Everett. But I don't think anything of it because Everett can also be particular. "One of the keys to shootin' doves for accuracy is knowing which ones to shoot at," he said to me one day last September. "Just like askin' a girl on a date. You gotta know which girl to ask so she doesn't say, no." Easy for Everett. What girl ever said no to him?

*

A pair of doves whiz over my head. I crouch down. They circle back. I shoot one dead as he's about to land and fire two shots at the other as it flares and escapes. One bird out of three shots isn't a great dove average but I'll take it. I walk out and pick up the dead bird. And that's when they come. First in pairs. Then in flocks. I jog back to my stand in the Johnson Grass to hide. And then I fire. And fire. Reload and fire. Doves fly in every direction. This is a dove hunt. This is a flight. Dad fires away too. Coffee runs back and forth retrieving birds. I can barely reload my gun fast enough to shoot. I hear Dad's words in my head: "Follow through good and *point* that gun don't *aim* it. Shotgun ain't a damn rifle." I always try my best to do what Dad says. "Shoot with both eyes open, not with one squeezed shut."

Before I know it, I've gone through a box of shells, all twenty-five, and my game bag is heavy. I walk out and pick up a bird and look at the horizon. Sun is headed west for the Pacific. *Red sky at night, sailor's delight. Red sky in morning, sailor take warning,* I hum in my dad's gravel-voice. He smokes three packs of Marlboro Reds a day, and I do my best to sound old. Today the sky says, *All sailors take delight.*

I look down Everett's way. It's been a while since I heard that first shot. Maybe I got lost in the frenzy of the hunt and didn't hear him shooting. Maybe Ev limited out fast and took a nap. Maybe he's over there snoring away, waiting for me to finish.

But then the logic of Everett Redding moves in and I realize: *No, Everett Redding does not fall asleep hunting.*

You see, Everett was born into the proud lineage of the Redding family, one of prestige in Rio Vista, and the owners of over two-thousand acres of prime land. "Peat" dirt. Dirt rich in moisture and nutrients from thousands of years underwater.

"Everything grows in peat," Everett always said. "Even Johnson Grass."

In his Wranglers, denim shirt and lace-up boots

51

Scott Barry

(what Everett called "his uniform") all purchased at Perry's local hardware store, Everett worked his family's land after school, on weekends and all summer long with calloused hands and a perpetual grin frozen in the corner of his mouth.

That's how much Everett loved to farm. And hunt.

He was instinctive and brave. He required no coaxing like me. Sure, I was a decent shot, but my stomach always turned when it came time to grab a crippled bird and wring its neck or smash its head against the stock of my gun putting it out of its bloody misery.

Not Everett. I once heard an old-timer at the local breakfast joint, Wimpy's, say, "That Everett Redding might be the purest hunter I ever seen." Then another chimed right in and crowed, "Only kid 'round here I never heard a single cross word about too."

I always wished I could hunt like Everett—with a clear conscience. Or as Dad always said, "Lots of guys can shoot but not many guys can *hunt*."

Everett could do both.

He was the only person Dad ever let have a key to his gunroom behind our garage. Everett would stop by and we'd talk about girls and football while he took apart his gun or loaded shells on Dad's loader. "You oughta learn to take apart and clean a gun like Everett," Dad would say. "Kid's mechanically inclined. Bet he knows his way around a car too."

I struggled to change the oil in my truck.

*

I dump out the birds from my game bag and count

52

them. "Damnit, only six." I take a deep breath. The familiar scent of this place rushes into my lungs. I can almost taste it. The safflower stubble. Yellow and decaying. Smells like the old chalkboards at school. The dirt too. Gritty and earthen. I can even smell the slough's muddy water baking in the sun like some kind of sweet mold, as if mother nature dabbed its musty odor with maple syrup.

All these smells arrive on the breath of an Indian Summer breeze—what we call the *Delta Breeze* in our little farming town of Rio Vista deep in the Sacramento River Valley—and six doves or not, it's a good day.

I look up at a couple doves sitting side-by-side on the phone lines between Everett and me, cooing away. "Crazy birds."

Always figured only the bravest doves would sit there on the lines well within range, boldly swaying in the breeze without fear of getting shot. They must know we're not allowed to shoot at 'em because it damages the wires and is against the law.

During dove season the old-timers at Wimpy's have been heard to grumble, "Damn phone's out again. Some idiot kid shootin' doves off a wire."

Not this kid.

Though Dad has said more than once, "You see a dove *landing* or *taking off* from a wire, fire away."

Truth is, Dad's been known to shoot a dove sitting on a wire, a pole, even the ground. "How we did things back in the day," he says, "No good reason to stop."

*

53

I stuff the dead doves back in my game bag. *Wonder how many Everett shot?* Probably more than my six. Probably shot his limit in ten clean shots and took that nap. Took me a box of twenty-five shells to shoot six. Or maybe I was daydreaming through all his gunfire. I can daydream with the best of them. Sure, he's lying there dead asleep, the only hunter to ever kill a limit of doves without making a sound.

Classic Everett. The kid with the golden smile.

We'd spent many an afternoon just like this, crouched in a safflower field or hiding in a row of standing corn or holed up in a dried-out ditch waiting for a flight of doves. One day, Everett got up from his post and walked over to me. When he arrived at my *post of the moment*—I'd moved a good five times that afternoon—he said, "Whenever you move, a dove flies over the spot you just left. Just to remind you that *where you were may have been the best place to be.*"

Damnit, if Everett Redding wasn't always right. Never could figure how he knew that kind of thing or how he learned to talk like an adult before the rest of us had hair on our balls.

*

The sun finally kisses the horizon. Goodbye, sun. Enough, I decide. Time to go get Everett and call it a day. *Damn that kid. He'd spend all night in a field if you let him,* I think, walking toward his spot on the pole line, sky suddenly glowing orange. With each step I imagine the end of the hunt talk Everett, Dad and I are about to have. That talk where we sit on the tailgate of Dad's Ford sipping Pepsi (Coors for Dad) and recount each dove we shot with great detail. One straight overhead. A bitch of a dove diving behind us. *A double.* And how we'll say "set" instead of "sit" because that's the way hunters talk around here.

"I was settin' right there and that damn pair almost landed right on top of me."

I imagine how good it'll feel to speak in a simple and manly way. And not feel ignorant or behind or like you're from a small town and not the city.

Just me, Dad, and Everett hunting doves in a safflower field in September like Everett and I will be doing with our boys once we're grown and married and fathers. Sure, I'd be living in the city by then, we all knew that. "You're too book smart for this place, pal," Everett would say. But Everett would always be in Rio Vista and we'd always meet up on the first of September.

We both knew that too.

*

When I arrive at Everett's spot on the pole line, I find one empty shotgun shell. No dead birds or feathers or scattering of empties or Everett. Just a single empty shell. I pick it up. Its brass head is cool in the palm of my hand. It's been sitting here awhile.

I look at the ditch a few feet away. "Everett?"

I walk to the ditch, stand at the edge and look to the bottom. Automatic, I suppose, to walk to a ditch, look down and see what's there. Usually, it's brown irrigation water or caked up mud or a mess of cattails and Johnson Grass. Once in a while if you walk up real quiet, you'll catch sight of something crawling around, a muskrat, a fox, maybe a gopher kicking dirt out of a hole. But not today.

Lying at the bottom of that ditch is Everett Redding, flat on his back, water up to his ears, eyes open. Wide.

For a second, I don't move. For a second, it seems, my breath stops. For a second, I do nothing—until I crash into the ditch with a thud and a splash. I don't touch Everett or try to speak to him or anyone else. No one else is there. It's only us. I stand over him. Still. For seconds it seems. For hours it seems. Staring at his eyes. I'd never seen this look in his eyes before. I'd never seen Everett Redding surprised about anything.

And then my eyes hit the shallow water—*blood red water*—but I don't scream or yell or lunge or do anything.

I do nothing. But wonder about that surprised look in his eyes.

My knees buckle but I resist until the weight of my body forces my knees into the slop, muddy water seeping through my jeans. The water feels cool against my skin.

I'm in the ditch now. At the *bottom*. With Everett. A cool drop of sweat rolls down my back. This isn't a dream. Or a nightmare. This is real life. I can feel it.

I lean toward Everett, my hands pushing into the mud. My ear almost touches his lips. I listen. To nothing. I listen harder. Is that possible? To listen harder? Still to nothing.

I touch his pale cheek with the back of my hand like my grandmother used to touch mine when I was under the spell of high fever. Soft. Cold. The air around us is thick with gnats and mosquitoes.

I try to stand with a hand against the wall of the ditch. But these walls are steep. I may never get out of this bloody ditch without the help of a friend. The only friend I have, here, is Everett. Everett Redding with a hole in his chest the size of my fist. My fist that's covered with globs of mud and blood and on seeing the globs, I stand up straight and somehow climb the steep bank on my hands and knees and belly. I climb not like a boy but like a wounded animal, fingernails desperately digging into dirt like claws.

At the top of the ditch I crawl through a patch of nettles that usually stings and makes me wince. I don't wince. Up on my feet I see Dad's truck—dark blue against the fading red sky—sitting at the end of the safflower field near a rusted metal barn. Why are all the barns here metal? Barns are supposed to be made of wood.

And then, eyes locked on Dad's Ford, I rise from the ground and float across the safflower field. Yes, I'm *floating* now, above the dirt and safflower stalks, beyond that ditch and Everett. The earth passing below me. And it feels good to float, to fly. My body—once heavy is now light. Me, not of the earth, not on the earth, but above it, floating toward Dad and away from Everett Redding.

*

It was then I knew Everett was never meant to see eighteen—and why. He'd become far too content much too early in life. Around here contentment is a mortal sin. Around here life is supposed to be hard.

It seems logical now. It didn't then. That is, if it were kids like me who didn't make it to eighteen there wouldn't

57

be all those mighty tunes about the 'good dying young.' Not that I was bad—but Everett Redding was *perfect*. Perfect in body, perfect in mind, perfect in spirit, perfect at farming and *perfect* at hunting.

Until his shotgun blew a hole in his chest that day.

Or as Sheriff Dixon said in his report, after a "thorough" investigation: "Everett slipped trying to jump the ditch." An irrigation ditch designed to carry water from the slough to the crops, while also dividing the fields into squares and rectangles that we call "checks." But this was no ordinary ditch; no, this was a rogue ditch with steep banks and a wide berth. Wide and steep and deep. Sometimes farmers clear out the ditches with backhoes, and the banks get so steep that even a dog can't get out without pulling on its collar. And if you're not there to pull on that collar, your dog might drown in the ditch, especially in the winter when the water is high. It's been known to happen. And if you fall in yourself, which also happens from time to time, you might need the hand of a friend to get out.

Somehow, I got out.

Sheriff Dixon added, "When Everett slipped, his gun somehow went off." One of the first lessons of Hunter Safety is always unload your gun before jumping a ditch or climbing a fence. It went off, he said, and "shot Everett in the chest." Or rather, Everett shot *himself* in the chest. Not intentionally but "accidentally."

*

Now, a Mexican ranch hand later told folks in town that he saw me stumbling and crawling across the safflower field, but I prefer to think he was telling a white lie, not out of meanness or to cause any harm, but because that's what people do in small towns to pass the time. Yes, he must have been lying, because I'm certain I was floating across that field that day.

Another farmer driving up on the levee road told the old timers at Wimpy's, "Kid ran like a bat out of hell *clean* to the end of that field and right up to his dad sitting there on the tailgate of his truck picking feathers from a dove like nuthin' but another day."

"Jesus, where the hell ya been?" Dad claimed he said when I arrived. Then seeing the blood: "What the hell? You okay? Where's Everett?"

But I don't remember Dad saying a single word. I just remember floating.

Dad said I also began trembling, and convulsing, and slobbering and spewing pieces of words. Apparently, I even puked on his favorite hunting boots. But he never said a word about that September day to me. Ever. Even a year later when he knew *he* was dying—not in the natural sense, but in the terminal Marlboro Red sense—did he ever say anything about that day to me.

"Life is hard, kid, just how it is," he said one afternoon before he took his last breath.

I knew, though, because people were talking about it at the post office, at Wimpy's, even at Hap's Bait Shop when I was in buying clams to go catfishing, Dad had said *something* to *someone.* Probably over a whiskey and soda at Tony's. Dad always lost the bitter grip on his mouth after a few whiskeys.

But to this day, they say, the people of Rio Vista—

and this much is believable—I spit out enough information to find Everett, and Dad did. They also say a sound came out of me. Some say it was a 'rebel yell'. Some say it sounded like that awful scream you hear in horror movies. But most said it sounded like a dying jackrabbit.

I don't remember making any kind of sound, though the jackrabbit part sounds like something Dad would say. A dying jackrabbit in the jaws of a dog is known to let out a scream that sounds worse than a baby desperately screaming for its mother.

Ma, ma! Ma, ma!

Once, after hearing that awful sound from a jackrabbit seconds from death in Coffee's mouth, I swore to Dad that I'd shoot Coffee or any dog that tried to kill a jackrabbit—before I would ever hear that sound again.

But they say, the day Everett Redding shot himself, I screamed like a dying jackrabbit.

HANK BEFORE SUNRISE

Most mornings I let Hank out around five-thirty and back in when he scratches at the door around six. He spends his half-hour of freedom in the orchard, relieving himself, then sniffing around for rabbits, fox, gophers, anything living or dead that tempts his great nose.

Hank's a hell of a hunting dog. Doesn't mind the cold. Loves the water. Has a soft mouth. Listens, most of the time. Even has a set of eyes so keen he'll spot ducks a hundred yards up, working the blind, wings cupped, necks craning to find just the right spot to splash down.

Hank's smart. He knows what comes next: gun fire, then Mallard, Sprig, Teal, and on a lucky day, Canadian Geese falling from the sky. Hank's so smart sometimes he'll beat a dead goose to the water.

*

While Hank's in the orchard I sit at the island in the kitchen with my smokes and a cup of coffee. The cooking vent above the island sucks up the smoke. That time of morning is good, too, since the wife's still asleep and can't hassle me. "Still smokin' on one goddamned lung," she'd say if she were up. Sure, she'll smell the hint of smoke when she gets up, but I'll have the vent turned up on high and the window opened good. And, besides, she'll have cursed me when I'm not around, and feeling better about having said it, won't need to repeat it to my face.

One day, though, after mowing the lawn and dumping the clippings in the orchard, she found a pile of butts under a cherry tree.

"Who the hell's been smokin' out in the orchard?!"

We both knew who'd been smoking in the orchard, and that that was her way of telling me to quit. We also both knew it wouldn't do any good. Already tried patches, gum, hypnotism, even those electronic cigarettes. But sitting there in a duck blind for hours when the sky is empty of birds, well, damnit, it's tough to quit. When I started back up smoking after the surgery, people around town gossiped that I had some kind of death wish but I just like to smoke. Even Dr. Barnes shook his head at me like I was a misbehaving child, wondering how in the hell having my ribs cut open, my left lung lopped off, followed by a week of hell in intensive care didn't do the trick.

"Can't really say, Doc," I coughed. "Pretty tough quittin' during duck season."

On hunting days, Wednesday, Saturday and

Hank Before Sunrise

Sunday—you never want to over-hunt a pond—I let Hank out early, around five or so. He knows it's a hunting day and is wound so tight that if I didn't let him out, he'd never be able to sit still on the fruit box I keep for him next to the blind. Around six we'll head over and pick up hunting-partner, Alan, and get to the pond around six-thirty. You can legally start to shoot a half-hour before sunrise and it can be the best time of the day—since the ducks can't see you so well and won't flare so damn easy.

*

It's still dark out. I look at my watch. Five to six. It's cold, with a good breeze from the north. Ducks fly lower when the wind is up and always against the wind when working the blind. I call Hank from the front porch a couple of times and wait. When he doesn't come running, I walk down the driveway to the edge of the cherry orchard and call him again. Still no Hank. I walk a few rows in, "Hank! Come!"

Back in the house the wife is up. "Where's Hank?" she asks. The woman's a human alarm clock. On Wednesday, Saturday and today, Sunday, she expects to hear me call Hank around six, then drive off a few minutes later.

"Don't know," I say. "Think I'll drive out back, see if he took off after a jack rabbit or somethin'."

Out back would be the alfalfa field past the first ditch at the end of the cherry orchard.

*

I've got my window down calling Hank from my truck. "Hank! Hank!" I look at my watch. Six-ten. Damnit, we're gonna miss the first morning flight when all the hunters head for their blinds, rousting all the overnight birds. You'll always get a fly-over shot or two first thing in the scramble of waking ducks.

I drive both side roads and all the way to the canal out back. Goddamn that Hank can be stubborn as hell sometimes. If he catches wind of a jack rabbit, he'll chase it all the way to town.

Back at the house I tell the wife I'm going hunting anyway and to let Hank in when he scratches at the door. She nods, smoking her one menthol cigarette of the day out the kitchen window, that for reasons I still can't figure, doesn't count like mine. Woman loves to eat, though, that's for sure. I've always eaten like a bird.

When I pull onto the highway it's six-twenty and I know Alan will be wondering what the hell's going on. I'm never late for a hunt. About fifty yards onto the highway I see a clump of something. Skunks are always wandering onto the highway and getting smashed and stinking up the whole world, so I swerve to my left to keep that horrible stink off my truck. But as I get closer the clump gets bigger, until I'm right next to it and know it ain't no skunk.

I back up onto the shoulder and keep my headlights on. I push in the cigarette lighter and reach for a smoke in the console, but realize I'd left them at home like I promised the wife. I climb out of my truck and start for the clump. At about ten feet out I know the clump isn't a skunk. It's too damn big. Maybe a coyote. But coyotes are browner and grayer than they are black, at least around here. I stop a step

64

away. Gotta be a dog. But the next ranch over is a good half-mile away. Maybe it's a stray, they come around once in a while. I circle the clump. Half its head is torn off and all that's left of its body are its neck and shoulders. I'm not sure where the rest of it is. Probably hit and torn to pieces by a big-rig and scattered on the road. Trucks haul corn this time of year and, hell, those rigs are so damn big and heavy when hauling a couple tons of corn, the driver probably thought he hit a skunk.

Dumb dog. Dumb fucking dog. Should've never let him out in the first place.

I always carry a shovel in the back of my truck. Habit when you live in the country. Seems you're always digging your way or somebody else's way into or out of something. Wish I carried a flat-head shovel. Works better on pavement.

I shovel Hank into a pile just off the side of the road and down the levee a bit where nobody would see him but where I could get to him later. I climb back in my truck and head for Alan's house. He has his dog, Cutter, an old Yellow Lab, and even though she's getting creaky and can't hunt everyday she's fine to get anything we shoot today.

When Alan climbs in the truck he says, "Where's Hank?"

"Dumb dog ran out back chasing a rabbit," I say. "Who knows."

"Hell, then, Cutter'll get a good workout today," he says, jumping out of the truck and walking back up his driveway. I turn the radio to the morning news. After helping Cutter into the back of the truck, Alan climbs into the cab and pulls out his thermos. "Coffee?"

When we pull off the two-lane paved road onto the

dirt access road, I know it's going to be a good hunting day. Flocks of ducks are in the sky with their calls filling the air, and the breeze is still going strong. Only thing better would be rain. Rain combined with wind really brings 'em down low.

We park my truck at the bottom of the slough levee about fifty yards from the small dyke that holds the water in our pond. It's a manmade pond. After the corn harvest most farmers in these parts, like the Mora family who owns this dirt, get in their green John Deere tractors and kick up berms around a field and pump slough water in to flood the fields. Pushes the salt down and nourishes the soil. The bay's not far off and salt's bad for any crop, especially corn. Been hunting this same spot for a good twenty years. Known the Moras for twice that.

Alan and I hop out of my truck, pull on our waders, grab our guns and bamboo walking sticks and head for the blind. You always need a walking stick to check for the small irrigation "spud" ditches that line the center of the pond. Step in one and you'll sink up to your waist in a second. Spud ditch shouldn't kill a man, but step into a main feeder ditch or a borrow pit and you're a goner. We've all heard stories about some dumbass duck hunter who stepped into a ditch with his waders on, how they filled up with water before he could get them off, and how he sank to the bottom like a lead weight. You'd read about that kind of thing at least once a year in the River News Journal. Usually, some dumbass from the city callin' himself a hunter.

Our blind is a two-seater brush blind with a dog box, a wooden fruit box with a canvas sack over it. Cutter climbs up on the box. We set it up a month or two before the season and before the Moras pump the slough water in. The water is up to our calves when we're sitting on our wooden seats.

Starting at about ten yards, and out to about forty yards, we set up our decoys. About a hundred of them. I always set one at fifty yards or so to gauge distance if we're hunting on a foggy day. Fifty yards is about the range of our shotguns. I've killed birds farther, but any hunter will tell you that's a one-in-ten shot. Standing tall in the middle of our decoys is a Robo Duck, a plastic duck decoy with a set of spinning wings run by a battery that's so lifelike it's damn deadly on ducks. Robos are so deadly you're only allowed to use 'em during the second half of the season when the birds begin to spook from seeing so many of their friends getting shot dead.

The blind is made of wooden stakes wrapped with chicken wire and dead and yellow stalks of Johnson Grass woven in the wire so that it looks like the weeds and grass around the ditch. Once we get in the blind and settle in, we load our guns and start searching the sky and calling with our duck calls. I do most of the calling. I've always had a knack for it. Most days, birds show up right off when I give a call. You think they'd know the difference. The same happens today. First a pair of Mallard high, then a dozen Sprig looking for a spot to land. I look over at Hank's box and want to tell him to sit. He always gets antsy first thing in the morning. Man, that dog loved to hunt. Cutter is there now, old and gray around the snout.

I miss the buck Mallard on my side but Alan knocks the hell out of the hen. Cutter takes her time picking it up, but she's a good dog and brings the bird back dead as hell. "Man, that one felt good," Alan says.

67

"Never got my gun up on my shoulder right," I say.

A flock of Sprig circle back on my call, work our blind and try to land in the decoys. When we stand, they flare into the sky, and we pull our triggers. This close we should get at least three, four, maybe five birds. Alan knocks down two and cripples a third that sails a hundred yards. I empty my gun. Normally, I'd curse and light up a cigarette for missing that bad, but I sit down and reload.

"Goddamn, I'm on fire," Alan says, stepping out of the blind as Cutter jumps in the pond after the two dead birds. "Gonna see if I can get that cripple," he hollers, taking off down the ditch.

I stand up to watch him. About sixty yards out he stops and takes a shot on the water. I see Cutter take off. Bird must be dead now.

Alan hangs all three Sprig on the duck strap and now we have four. The limit is seven a man, but you can only shoot two Sprig a piece and up to seven Mallard. One of the Sprigs starts to flop and wiggle, and Alan grabs it and slams its head against the butt of his shotgun. Some blood squirts onto the arm of my jacket. He hangs the bird back on the strap, pink tongue hanging out of its yellow bill.

I don't shoot at the next flock of Mallards and Alan pops two more birds. "I'm on goddamn fire," he says, then looks at me. "Why ain't you shootin'? What the hell's got into you?"

"Hank's dead," I say.

"What?"

"Lying in a pile of fucking fur and blood and guts on the side of the road just down from the house."

"Hank's dead? Thought he was just chasin' a rabbit."

"Fuck's the matter with you? Didn't hear me the first fucking time. He's dead."

Now, most men in our small farming town of Isleton wouldn't let themselves be talked to like that by another man, but Alan knows me, and I know him and, well, it's just how we talk to each other sometimes.

"What the hell happened?" he says.

"Figure he got hit by an eighteen-wheeler hauling corn on the levee road. Dumb dog. Dumb fucking dog. Probably chased a rabbit. Shoulda never let his dumb ass out in the first place."

Alan looks at Cutter, old and gray around the snout. "But you let him out every damn morning. What the hell?"

"What's the goddamned difference? Shoulda never let him out in the first place."

"That's a goddamned shame," Alan says. "Sorry to hear that. Hank was a goddamn good hunting dog."

I look at the dead ducks hanging from the strap. What the hell are we doing out here anyway? Shooting a bunch of ducks that are just stopping for a swim and a bite to eat. Filling them full of lead, steel now, since you can't shoot lead anymore. Hauling them home, picking their feathers out in the orchard, singeing the baby feathers with a blow torch, stinking up the whole world with the smell of burning feathers, then gutting them and cutting off their wings, head and feet, and either throwing them in the oven right then or freezing them in plastic bags for some other time.

 What the hell?

"I gotta get home," I say. "Hank's lying there on the side of the road. Ain't right."

Hank, the only dog I ever let sleep on the bed or on

the ottoman in front of my chair. He was like a damn kid. He'd hang his head and limp around when he didn't get to go for a ride in the truck—when all the time we both knew there wasn't anything wrong with his damn leg. Nobody ever believed me when I'd tell them about the act Hank would put on until they'd come by and I'd say 'watch this.' I'd get into the truck without pulling the tailgate down for Hank, start her up, and he'd go into his routine of hobbling and limping around and whining. Craziest thing I ever saw. What a dog, what a goddamned great dog. Always laying his head in your lap. Looking at you with the eyes of a boy.

Dumb fucking dog. What the hell was he doing up on the highway anyway?

Alan lights a cigarette. "Tell you what," he says, "have a smoke and think about it. Maybe you'll feel better after a good hunt."

Alan offers me one of his Marlboro Reds and clicks his lighter. He's right, it does feel good, smoke dragging across the back of my throat and into my one good lung. Alan doesn't say a damn thing about me smoking or my missing a lung. He likes to smoke too much himself. He used to give me a case of Marlboro Reds every year for Christmas until Dr. Barnes told me I had cancer, and then all the surgery and intensive care. But Alan still gives me one of his when we're hunting. He also likes who I am when I smoke. I can be a goddamn asshole when I'm not smoking, biting the head off any sonofabitch who doesn't deserve it. But, when I smoke, I don't do that stuff.

"What'ya think?" he says. "Wanna stay out?"

"Hell." I exhale. "Let's give it a half-hour or so."

Hank Before Sunrise

*

Another pair of Mallard works the blind and comes so damn close on the first pass that I see the Buck's green head clear as spring grass. We crouch down, ready to shoot.

"Let me know," Alan says.

The birds are on my side, so it's my call. They come in against the wind, wings cupped. Goddamn they're beautiful birds.

"Take 'em!"

Alan's up quick. He stones the hen on the first shot. I'm behind on the buck and he climbs hard for the sky. On the second shot I nick him in the ass and clip one of his wings on the third. He tumbles end-over-end before spiraling into the pond. I know he'll be alive when I get to him. And if he has a chance, he'll dive.

Ducks will do that, go down and hang onto a corn stalk and drown themselves before they'll let you catch 'em. Never could figure that. They'd rather die than be captured. Like noble warriors in some ancient battle with man. But Hank would always find them. Dog had a nose like nothing I'd ever seen.

Alan sends Cutter out to get the hen and I climb out of the blind and head for the buck. He hollers at me to let Cutter get the buck too, but I can't hear him. All I can hear is a big rig tearing apart Hank up on the levee road. Dog couldn't have suffered. He was dead in an instant, sure, but I can't stop wondering what it sounded like, and if I'd heard it if I hadn't had the vent on. Thought I heard a truck or two go by, though you hear them all the time, especially this time of year. But a hundred pounds of the finest Black Lab I'd ever seen smashed against the chrome bumper of semi, man, that had to make some kind of sound.

*

The green head is barely alive when I get to him. I wait a second to catch my breath, wheezing like a goddamn old man. Sure, I'd just trudged through a hundred yards of mud and water and over a good six or seven spud ditches, but damnit if I don't sound like I'm dying.

The Mallard didn't dive, he couldn't; his wing's broken almost in half. He's lying there on his side, one eye staring at me. Wonder what the hell I look like to him? Some monster come to end his life? I grab him by the neck and smash his head against the butt of my gun. He's still twitching so I smash his head again and again and again and again till blood and brains drip from the butt of my shotgun.

*

"Helluva shot," Alan says as I toss the Mallard into the blind. "Shit, you almost took off his head."

"Got him on the third shot."

"Damn, you set that pattern right on his nose. Helluva shot."

"Let's go," I say. "Gotta get Hank off that damn levee before some coyote chews him up."

"You sure? We only need a couple more birds."

"I'm sure."

*

Hank Before Sunrise

When I drop off Alan, he knows I won't be hunting for a while. Probably not for the rest of the season. He knows he'll go by himself to pull out our blind and decoys when the water recedes and the ground dries in the spring and that I'll thank him when he does. He'll never say another word about Hank. Why would he? When his own son nearly died from a brain tumor, he never said a word to me. I only found out about the kid's surgery when I ran into him at the post office, with his shaved head and ear-to-ear scar. "Lucky to be alive," his son said with a little laugh. But Alan never said a single word about it.

On the way home from Alan's, I stop by Peter's Hardware to buy a sheet of plastic. I toss it in the back of the truck. When I pull up, Hank's still lying by the side of the road. But it's light now, and I can't look at him too long.

*

I park near the oak grove out back behind the cherry orchard and dig a hole. My grandfather built a house out here back in the '40s for the Mexican family who worked the ranch. It's why there's a small clearing in the middle of the grove where the house once stood. I'm thankful to have my spade shovel now because despite the rain we've had these past couple weeks, the ground is hard. I dig a good, deep hole. Coyotes dug up the last dog I buried out here. Shot two of them dead with my rifle the next day.

I wrap what's left of Hank in the plastic and tie it tight around him with a strip of rope. I lower Hank into the hole. I start filling the hole, but my stomach aches so bad that I walk over to some bushes to puke but it's only dry heaves.

I walk back to Hank and light another cigarette Alan gave me "just in case." A couple of drags and my head feels light, like it's my first cigarette. The ground starts to spin. I take a knee to steady myself. I can barely breathe but I grab the shovel and push some dirt on Hank. I'm still dizzy. I get down on my other knee and pat the dirt hard with the shovel. Then with my hands.

What a dog. What a damn fine dog. I swear on my life if a coyote touches Hank I'll kill him and his whole damn coyote family.

*

"Where's Hank?" the wife asks when I walk into the kitchen, my knees and hands covered in mud.

"Hank's gone," I say. "Took him out back under the oaks."

"Oh," she says.

HEART OF JOANNE

Rehab is for losers and junkies who can't maintain and end up doing stupid shit, thinks Joanne, pacing while picking at the dried blood underneath her fingernails. Losers like Stuart, that puny bitch who thinks he has all the answers. Fucker. Only thing that ex-crackhead has is a pockmarked face and yellow teeth. And he's gonna help Joanne kick? Kick what? A couple sips of booze a day and a line of somebody's leftovers. Pills don't count. Hospitals give out worse. Besides, she can't feel a damn thing with pills anymore. *Might as well be fucking placebos.* Needles, sure, she can feel those, but shooting heroin too much fucks up your skin. Joanne loves her skin—at least she used to.

Joanne stops pacing and looks out the rain-streaked window of the clinic. *Fuck.* The cop car is still in the parking lot getting doused by a spring downpour. Fuck the cops. Fuck Stuart. Fuck rehab. Fuck withdrawal. The sweats, the puking, the shakes. Joanne has *been* through it all before. *Seen* it all before. Especially the sniveling degenerates who can't hack withdrawal and turn to God, blubbering on about shit lives and abuse. *Grow the fuck up*. If anyone knows abuse, it's Joanne. But she'll never tell her story. Why would she? Nobody gives a shit. Sure, the other patients will nod and conjure up warm smiles, maybe even pump out a few fake tears, but all everyone ever thinks about is themselves. *Always*. Especially the egomaniac counselor Stuart. When he shared that he contracted HIV from needles, Joanne kicked the floor. She was sure it was sex. Anal sex. Hardcore anal sex, the kind that made him grunt and bleed. At least she hoped it was.

"Nothing about that man would inspire a dog," Joanne whispered to a female patient over a cup of coffee after their first group meeting. "So what if he's positive? We supposed to feel sorry for him? Needles, sex, a transfusion? Who cares?"

Joanne turns away from the window and digs her lighter from her back pocket—even though she knows she can't smoke inside and Stuart won't let her out to the smoking area, so why even think about it? Because it makes her feel better to have the lighter in her hand, for one—just to feel it—and two, she likes the heat of the flame along her palm. At least it's real. The smell of burning butane, too, calms her, stops her hands from shaking, distracts her from the cut on her forehead, hidden under the hospital bandage. Her swollen lip also, thankfully, cut on the inside. Not on her skin.

Heart of Joanne

She clicks out a flame and inhales the fumes. If Michael would just fucking show up, Stuart would get his, including a front row view of Joanne's ass as she prances out the door; and prance she would, smiling and cackling; maybe even a double-flip of the bird that'd remind Stuart of his glory days in the '80s when his Billy Idol dye job shouted hip instead of homo.

Yes, out the door she would go. Her and her ass. If only the door to the meeting room weren't locked. If only Stuart didn't hold the key. If only the cops weren't waiting to hear what Michael had to say about all this. If only it would quit raining. If only Michael would hurry up and get his country ass here. But he's always late. Determined to drive Joanne insane.

She pockets the lighter and paces. "Fucking hell, Michael, where the *fuck* are you? People in Sacramento don't have a fucking clue how to drive in the rain. Fucking clueless!" It's been forty minutes since Stuart called the police and then Joanne called Michael, getting his voice mail, always his voice mail, always leaving a frantic message for him. "Take it easy, I was under a car and couldn't answer my phone," would be his first excuse. "Calm the fuck down, my hands were greasy," would be his second. "I'm a human fucking being, I was taking a crap," would be his third. Fuck Michael's simple country ass. He should've stayed in Clarksburg and baled hay with his dad and pumped out five kids with some ditzy country girl instead of moving to Sacramento with his hippie convert mom. Fuck his excuses.

*

Joanne stops and looks out the window again. Of course, it's still pouring rain. Of course, the two douchebags are still sitting in their cop car, sipping 7-11 coffee and bragging about their last crack whore blowjob. At least they finally turned off the flashing red light. As if it were an emergency. As if Joanne were a flight risk. As if she didn't swear on her daughter's life that it was a joke. A silly joke. But not to Stuart, he takes everything serious, most of all himself. "Intent to commit murder is a very serious matter, Joanne," he had said with his lisp and drama queen eyes all squinted when the cops first pulled up.

"You're so fucking gay that way," Joanne had shot back.

"I warned you that it would all get *worse* before it got *better.*"

"Fuck your psychobabble bullshit." Joanne had snarled. "You're nothing but a little snitch."

Joanne picks at her fingernails. Fuck the cops, too. Like they don't have anything better to do. How about solving one of the dozens of unsolved murders in the city?

"California law 5150: a counselor or therapist can detain a patient if he has reason to believe that patient may harm himself or someone else," the big cop had read as his partner put handcuffs on Joanne. She tuned him out and stared at his bulge, wondering if he had a big cock or just got off wearing tighty-whities so everything balled up in his polyester blue uniform.

*

Joanne walks to the other end of the room and the

78

water cooler. She grabs a paper cup from the dispenser. She fills it to the top. She gulps at the cool water, hoping to quench her dry mouth, her endless thirst. It's her only gripe about drugs: the destruction of her teeth and skin. She's convinced she'll have dentures and a face like a football by the time she's forty.

She crumples the cup in her hand as the water rolls across her tongue and down her throat and into her chest, and from there, God knows where. Her broken body begs to cry but she refuses. Instead, she leans her head back and screams, silently. Nobody comes. Why would they? She hasn't made a sound. Besides, she isn't on *suicide* watch, she's on *homicide* watch. She laughs at the thought, at the difference, at the absurdity of it all. Suicide or murder, who cares? Someone dies either way. We *all* eventually die.

Joanne walks back to the window. Her eyes widen and she clutches her hands at her heart. Michael's at the cop car. "Michael!" she screams through the window and pounds on the pane. "Michael!"

Michael squints through the rain at Joanne banging on the window. "Joanne?"

From Michael's vantage Joanne looks like a watery ghost, fists thundering away on the window.

"Goddammit, Michael, c'mon!"

The big cop looks at his watch, then pats Michael on the arm and nods. Joanne bounds to the door, squirms and waits. She wants to cry but knows it's too soon, that it won't get her out, yet. She'll need her tears later.

Joanne hears footsteps and voices in the hall. The knob turns, forever turning. Then the door opens, and Michael appears, wet and worried. "Joanne!" he says and closes the door behind him. He holds Joanne tight. So tight the water on his clothes seeps through her blouse and onto her skin. Her nipples harden; at least she can feel that.

"Michael," she says.

"Are you okay?" he asks.

"I'm fine."

"You sure?" he asks, and steps back to look at her.

"I'm sure. I'm positive." She notices the scratches on Michael's cheek as if for the first time. They've begun to heal like the cut on her forehead and the gash inside her mouth. She wonders if his scratches still sting like her cuts do when she's in the shower. Michael looks around the room for something to wipe his soaked hands with.

"What the hell's going on?" He finds a box of tissues and accidentally pulls a thick wad from the box. "Shit," he says, thinking what a waste it is to take more than you need of anything—even at a time like this.

"I'm sorry, I'm so sorry," Joanne says.

"It's okay," he says, tossing the soggy tissues in the trash can. "I got your message and raced out here. It's raining like hell. Fucking gridlock on the 50."

"I'm sorry," Joanne says.

"It's okay, I just . . . you scared me. And then they almost wouldn't let me in . . . they were talking some crazy shit . . . *intent to commit murder* . . . some sort of plan. They wouldn't say exactly. They wanted me to talk to you first."

"They're trying to set me up, Michael. And using you to do it."

"Set you up?"

"To see if my story *to you* matches my story *to them*."

"What story?"

"It's a crazy mess, Michael. All because of him."

"The big cop?"

"No. Stuart," Joanne says sharply.

"The little guy who just let me in? Same guy who checked you in?"

"Yeah, that fucking guy. Did you talk to him?"

"No, he just opened the door." Michael shrugs. "Didn't say much. Same as when we first showed up."

"Because he's in on it. It's a trap."

"Joanne, what the hell's going on?"

"It was supposed to be family night, and *he* went and screwed it all up," she says.

"That guy Stuart screwed it up? How could—"

"Where's Madeline? Is she okay?" Joanne says.

"Madeline's fine. She's with my mom."

"Does she know? Don't tell her. I'm not—"

"Don't worry, I'm not going to tell her...." Michael's voice drifts off. He looks at Joanne and squeezes the moisture from his beard. His thoughts turn into words. "Uh, what am I *not* going to tell her?"

Joanne takes Michael by the shoulders. "I'm not crazy, Michael."

"I know you're not crazy."

"The cops tried to tell you I was crazy, didn't they?"

Michael looks through the blinds at the cops sitting in their cruiser sipping their 7-11 coffee.

"They didn't really say it like that."

Joanne pirouettes, dramatically, like a dancer, gasping loud—then realizes she saw this move in her head moments before and had been waiting to use it. How strange and delicious to now pull it off.

Scott Barry

"Goddammit! I knew they would!" she says.

"Hey, I told them *they* were crazy," Michael says.

"I'm not crazy, Michael!" says Joanne, Michael's wife, stomping on the floor.

"Jo, look at me.... I know you're not crazy."

"I know . . . it's just that this time has been a lot harder than I thought it would be . . . and I think I've been hallucinating . . . and the shit I've been putting in my body the last ten years made me feel a helluva lot better than I feel right now."

"It's okay," Michael says and takes her by the shoulders. And now a tear does escape from her eye, slowly, a lonely tear.

"They put handcuffs on me, Michael." Joanne falls into Michael's arms, forcing an audible sniffle. She knows the image of her in handcuffs will get a rise from Michael and ignite his distrust of anyone wearing a uniform and wielding a stick.

"Handcuffs? The sonofabitches put handcuffs on you!" Michael looks at her, then at her wrists. "*Fucking hell. Why would they do something like that?!*"

"Michael, you need to talk to them, tell them that you believe me . . . that this is all a big misunderstanding."

Michael grits his teeth: "Fucking pigs."

He remembers his mother shouting the same at peace rallies at the state capitol when he was a kid. He always wanted to say it out loud and to a real pig's face. "Fine. Fine! They put fucking handcuffs on you!" Michael bounds for the door. He will defile these pigs, spit in their faces and if necessary be taken by force, dragging and kicking. How glorious to finally protest.

"And watch out for that little Nazi," Joanne says.

Michael stops. "Wait a minute. What am I going to tell them?"

"That you believe me."

"Right, 'that I believe you . . . '" Michael scratches at his temple. "But what do I believe you about?" Michael hates the fact that nothing can leave his mouth that he doesn't absolutely believe to be true. If only he could lie, at will, like Joanne.

"That I wasn't planning to murder anybody," Joanne says and clicks her lighter. Michael looks at the lighter. That sound chills him in a way he had never known until right now. Joanne slides the lighter back in her pocket. She knows the click was a mistake, a tell. Her first.

But there it is. The possibilities flash in Michael's blinking eyes. The damage Joanne could do. Was capable of. Not only to herself, but to others. A nurse, a counselor, that annoying roommate. It had all happened before—only not like this. Not this far. Not with murder.

"Murder?" Michael speaks finally. "Why would they think you were going to murder someone?"

"Because they have no sense of humor."

Michael steps back into the room. "Okay, slow down, I'm lost here. They think you're going to murder somebody because they 'have no sense of humor?'"

"It was a joke. *Killing someone*. They turned it into this ridiculous mess."

Michael takes a step forward. "You were *joking* about killing someone?"

"Michael, they're threatening to charge me with intent to commit murder."

"Intent to commit murder?" He half-laughs. "Someone specific or were you just *intending* to go on a random killing spree?"

"Michael, this isn't funny."

"No, you're right." He looks out the window. "So who'd they think you were intending to kill?"

"Who?"

"Yes. Who?" Michael says.

Joanne looks away. "It was all just a stupid joke."

"Then why are there cops all over the place?"

"All over the place? There's two idiots outside talking about pussy."

"Who?"

"It was a joke," Joanne says. "It doesn't matter."

Michael turns and paces the length of the room. He stops, eyes searching, his back to Joanne. "Fine, it doesn't matter."

"Fine."

Michael spins to Joanne. "*Fine?*"

"Michael, it's stupid. It doesn't matter."

"How could it not matter? This is a human being we're talking about."

Joanne reaches for her lighter but hesitates. "A human being in a hypothetical situation."

"Okay, so who were you talking about— *hypothetically*?"

"It doesn't matter!"

Michael holds his gaze on Joanne. She chews on her bottom lip. They both know it matters. It *all* matters when you've been married ten years and have a kid. Only one. Yes, every little thing matters, and Joanne knows it. She pulls another paper cup from the water cooler and pours from the dispenser. She downs it in a single gulp. She crumples the cup and tosses it toward the waste basket.

Michael watches the cup float through the air, spinning and tumbling in slow-motion until it lands with a thud.

"Fine," he says coolly. "It doesn't matter."

"Thank you," says Joanne, wiping her mouth with the back of her hand like a drunken cowboy before a fight. Michael had never seen that move from Joanne and doesn't like it.

"Now who was it?" he says.

"It doesn't matter."

"Jo, tell me who—"

"My husband! All right, goddammit! My husband!"

They stare at each other.

Michael takes off his coat and calmly lays it over the back of a chair. Joanne walks to the window to see outside, something, anything that has air and rain and moonlight.

Michael exhales, not as the man he is now but the one he was before all of this. "Joanne . . . I'm your husband."

Joanne goes to him, holds his face. The tears come for her now. Just like she knew they would.

"Michael, it's a mess. An absurd mess." She coughs. "Just tell them that you believe me . . . that I wasn't planning on . . . killing you."

Michael looks deep into Joanne's eyes, searching for anything but the darkness he sees. "Killing me?"

"That's what they think."

Michael nods. A thought forms in his head. He half-smiles with recognition. "So that was the plan," he says.

"The plan?" Joanne asks.

"The last thing the big cop said was, 'She had a plan.' I assumed you were thinking of . . . *planning on* . . . harming yourself."

"It wasn't really a *plan*."

"By the sound of the big cop's voice you were plotting an assassination," says Michael with a scratch of his beard.

Joanne knows the gesture. It's the second time he's done that. Suspicious thoughts have infiltrated Michael's head and Joanne must erase them.

"That's what police do, Michael. They go around giving ridiculous stuff official names. It makes them feel important. And besides, it wasn't really a *plan*. A plan is something you're *actually planning to do*."

"Okay. So, what was the unofficial plan that you weren't *planning to do*—that involved me dead and not you?"

Joanne sighs.

"It's completely ridiculous, Michael."

Michael nods, sits in the chair, crosses his legs and folds his arms. He wants Joanne, his wife, *his wife who joked about killing him*, to know that he will not leave or speak to the cops or Stuart the counselor or anyone else until she quits *fucking* around and stops acting like the junkie she is and tells him the goddamned truth.

"I'm sure it's ridiculous," he says evenly. "In fact, I'm certain of it. You were kidding. You have a habit of doing that. I believe you. So what was the plan?"

"What was it?"

"Hypothetically."

"Hypothetically?"

"Unofficially," he says.

Joanne can barely contain her impulse to shout it out, marvel at her audacity. "It's so ridiculous I don't even wanna say it."

"Just tell me. We'll have a good laugh and we'll settle this whole thing."

"You might not think it's so funny," she says.

"Joanne, the thought of you planning to kill me is funny—sort of."

"See, right there . . . "

"I promise I'll laugh."

"It's absurd, it's—"

"I promise."

"You promise?"

"With my life." He traces a "x" over his heart and manages a smile. "Cross my heart."

Joanne thinks about how to say this. Now. Now that Michael who never asks questions about anything other than the weather suddenly isn't being Michael. Just like he wasn't himself when he backhanded her four days ago in a fit of rage, gashing the inside of her mouth. And Joanne, fueled with every bit of her angry self, punched him in the side of the head and clawed at his cheek so he'd never *fuck with her again*.

"All right, fine," she says, "we were in the middle of a group session…. The 'sacred circle of life' or whatever Stuart calls it . . . and the guy sitting next to me starts on some fairy tale about being suicidal . . . even said how he planned to do it."

"How?"

"Carbon monoxide."

"That's a fairy tale?"

"The guy doesn't own a car."

"How do you know that?"

"Because he said it right there, 'But I don't have a car.' I mean, first you gotta have a car . . . or at least access to a car *and* a garage . . . before you can do something like that . . . even think about it."

"I suppose," Michael says.

Joanne begins pacing now, the thought of TV attorneys and melodramatic closing arguments drifting into her head. "So anyway, I throw myself on the floor in a hysterical fit. I don't know why. The whole thing . . . this place . . . just seemed so pointless. And the next thing you know, the little shit who runs the place, bitchy Stuart, asks me in a super condescending tone: 'Are you suicidal, Joanne?' And I say, 'No . . . but I'm *homicidal*!' I thought it would make everyone laugh. I almost peed myself."

"Homicidal?"

"Yeah."

"Killing someone?"

"Right."

"The taking of a life?"

"That's what *homicide* is, Michael."

"And this just happens to be the part where I came in?"

"Yeah, right about there . . . " she says.

"Okay," he says.

"So, anyway, I said, 'In fact, I've been entertaining the thought of killing my husband.'"

"You have?"

"Who hasn't?"

"Thought about killing their spouse?" Michael says.

"You've never thought about killing me?"

"No."

"Never even *entertained* it?"

"*Entertained* it?"

"For a split second?"

"No," Michael says. This is what Joanne's always loved most about the Michael she knows. The one she can do with what she pleases—even when she's wrong.

Joanne walks to the window and turns her back to Michael to let him know that she *knows* he's lying. Michael who never lies.

"C'mon, Michael, even the time I hocked your Fender Strat' for some dope? Even then?" Michael's eyes laser in on the back of Joanne's selfish head. *Fuck her.* He loved his green Fender Stratocaster his mother gave him for his sixteenth birthday.

"Yeah . . . maybe the Fender. Maybe I thought about it for a split second."

"Thank you," Joanne says, turning triumphantly. Michael looks away at nothing. She begins pacing again. "So, anyway, Stuart says, 'How?' You know, 'How are you gonna do it, Joanne?"

"The plan?" Michael asks.

"Yeah, the plan."

Michael uncrosses and crosses his legs. He squeezes his arms into his chest. He fumes at the thought of his Fender sitting in the window of some pawnshop on Del Paso Boulevard, grimy amateur hands fondling it, paying half its value to get played badly in some cover band's beer bottle garage. His blood boils. "How'd you get on the subject?"

"The carbon monoxide guy that doesn't have a car."

"Right," he says.

"But the whole time I'm thinking this guy's fulla shit."

"Which guy?"

"Both of them really," Joanne says. "But I'm talking about Stuart, the leader of the cult." She tucks her hair behind her ears, confidence building. "So, I figure he's playing the therapist routine, which you know how much I hate." Michael sighs because he knows. Joanne continues. "On top of that I'm starting to get the shakes, so I figure I'll give him something, you know, to think about. So, I say, 'Fuck yeah, as soon as I get outta here I'm gonna kill 'im."

"Me again."

"Right. And I say, 'I'm gonna go to Home Depot, buy me some rat poison and put it in his stew."

"Stew? You can barely make a salad," Michael says.

"Exactly."

"That's a helluva an imagination you have."

"You promised you'd laugh."

"I'm working up to it."

"Well, next thing you know I'm going on about how I've been 'planning it for years' . . . how I'm gonna 'take the life insurance money.'"

"We don't have life insurance."

"I know that, but Stuart doesn't. So, I'm—"

Michael stands. "Rat poison?"

"Yeah, rat poison."

"How do you know they sell rat poison at Home Depot?" he asks.

"Where else would you get it?"

"I don't know . . . most people don't know Home Depot carries rat poison and sells it over the counter. Especially people like you who've never been to Home Depot."

"So I guessed right. Who cares?"

Michael inhales. "So, if you were going to kill me, you'd kill me with rat poison?"

"I'm not going to kill you, Michael. This whole thing was a joke. Hello! Did you miss that part?"

"Well, obviously, that's not what the cops think."

"That's because they talked to Mr. Squeaky Ass."

"That's a helluva thing to joke about."

"Michael, you said you've thought about killing me."

"But I never went so far as to *entertain* a plan."

"Oh, come on, you've never fantasized about pushing me down a flight of stairs . . . maybe giving me a little nudge into traffic . . . maybe an unexpected boost over the railing off the I Street Bridge . . . watch me splash into the river? I'm a terrible swimmer and you know it."

"Listen to you."

"It'd be a simple thing to do, and you'd probably get away with it."

"Get away with it?"

"Oh, c'mon, Michael, admit it. You haven't just thought about killing me, you've thought about *how* you'd kill me."

"I have not!"

"It's entirely natural."

"It is not!"

"You have!"

91

"I haven't!"

"Even when I hocked your Fender?!"

"All right! Fine! I might've thought about smothering you *after you hocked my goddamned Fender*! There? Happy?" Michael takes a breath and grinds his palms together. Fuck. Did he say that out loud? Sure, he thought about smothering that condescending smirk off Joanne's face after she hocked his beloved Fender *that his dead mother gave him!* Joanne, who would flail and claw at him as he pressed harder and harder until her eyes exploded from her head and she let out her last agonizing breath. What freedom he would know!

Joanne turns away, eyes searching. "*Smother me?* Michael, that's sick . . . that's awful."

"Sick? Compared to rat poison, smothering seems pretty humane."

"Please tell me we're not having this conversation."

"But rat poison . . . " says Michael as Joanne covers her ears like she'd seen their daughter Madeline do when being asked to clean her room, " . . . that's gotta be a horrible death . . . fucking Hitchcock shit!"

Joanne closes her eyes. She's reached that place where she might launch herself out the window of the clinic, a clean white sheet tied around her neck. But when she opens her eyes, they meet Michael's hateful glare. No. She will not melt like all those degenerate addicts who turn to God and confess sins they haven't committed only to paint themselves as victims armed with manufactured dramas designed to receive sweet empathy from the group. No, Joanne will not be weak like them.

"Okay, fine," she says and marches to the door. "I'm

gonna get Stuart, the little shit who runs this place, the jerk who prodded me into this mess, the rat who turned me into the police, the drama queen who made a big deal out of nothing and you can decide for yourself."

Joanne opens the door knowing that Stuart is exactly the kind of person Michael loathes most, snooty and pretentious and arrogant, an intellectual bully, constantly spouting wisdom-pearls stolen from this or that self-help book as if they were his own. Michael despises all that self-help wisdom shit gained by a book, or a *hand* on a book, or a prayer, or kneeling before God—and not from living with greasy hands on the steering-wheel of your own fucking life.

Michael walks to the window and stares at the cops. "Are there enough fucking sports in the world for you guys to talk about all night, driving around sipping crappy coffee?"

The door opens but Michael doesn't bother to turn around. Joanne walks up behind him, arms folded. "Okay, Michael, here he is."

Michael exhales and turns to find the extended hand of Stuart.

"Hi, I'm Stuart," Michael reluctantly shakes his hand.

"Michael."

"We sort of met in the hall," Stuart says. "And the other day."

"Nice to *officially* meet you," Michael says. He already doesn't like Stuart, and Joanne can tell. Stuart and Michael look at each other a moment waiting for the other to speak.

"You're a very lucky man, Michael," Stuart says

Scott Barry

finally. "Very lucky . . . " Michael's questioning eyes prompt Stuart to finish the thought, " . . . to be alive."

Joanne scoffs, looks at Michael. "*See.*"

Stuart tightens his jaw. This is his clinic. *His*. The place where all his sins have been washed away. He will not be mocked by anyone, least of all Joanne. "Expressed intent to commit murder is a very serious matter, Joanne," he says.

"Listen, she's been under a lot of pressure," Michael says.

"You're damn right I have. Stuart, tell Michael how it was all just a little joke that's turned into a big misunderstanding and we can settle this and go home."

"I didn't think you were joking, Joanne."

"How could you not think I was joking? I'm gonna poison my husband?"

"This may come as a surprise to you, Joanne, but this isn't the first time I've dealt with something like this."

"I thought this whole thing was supposed to be anonymous anyway."

"You're thinking of confidentiality," Stuart says.

"What's the difference?" Joanne asks as Michael watches, fascinated with this two-headed creature called 'Joanne and Stuart.'

"We follow the same rules as therapists," Stuart says.

Joanne scoffs. "Hard as you try, and you try really hard, you're obviously not a therapist."

"No, but I am a Certified Alcohol and Drug Abuse Counselor."

"Right, you were a junkie, you did a lot of shitty stuff, you feel guilty about it, so now you're a counselor."

"This isn't AA, Joanne. This is a residential

94

treatment center where we're required to follow the same rules as therapists when it comes to issues of harm...." Stuart looks at Michael. "Including murder."

"Murder," Michael says as much to himself as anyone.

"Michael, I'm not going to *murder* you."

Michael tugs on his beard. Stuart and Joanne. Michael and Joanne. Michael and Joanne and Madeline their daughter. He turns to Stuart. "How did she say it when she said it?" Michael asks.

"Michael!" Joanne says.

"Excuse me?" Stuart asks.

"You know, the inflection and all."

"Very convincingly," Stuart says.

"Aren't you being just a *little* dramatic?" Joanne says.

"Did she say it like she meant it?"

"Michael, have you lost your mind!"

"At the time," Stuart says, "it seemed like she meant it."

"I didn't mean it, you smug little shit!"

"You said you were *entertaining* the thought of killing your husband. You used the word 'entertain.' That's like people putting a smiley face next to their signature. It's the mark of a sociopath."

"*A sociopath!*" Joanne wails.

"I'm not saying you're a sociopath per se, I'm not qualified to make that determination," Stuart says, enjoying the simple act of saying the word. "I'm making a general point that you've exhibited sociopathic tendencies."

Joanne can no longer take this. This mutant named

Stuart. She will wrap her hands around his puny neck and crush his skull and stomp his brains into Jell-O. She steps closer to Stuart, index finger inches from his face.

"I bet everybody you know is a used-to-be something: crackhead, boozer, junkie. News flash: there's a whole world out there where people kid about all kinds of stupid shit including *killing someone,* like, you know, *'I'm gonna fuckin' kill you!'* and it doesn't literally mean *they're going to fucking kill you!*"

"We've been through this, Joanne. You entered the zone of perpetration and you know it." Stuart walks to the door. "I would appreciate it if you two would settle this as soon as possible. I can't shut down the whole program while you work out your problems. I'm not a marriage counselor."

Joanne turns to Michael. "Let's get the fuck outta here."

Michael looks at Stuart. "What's the 'zone of perpetration'?"

Stuart stops at the door and suppresses a smile. He'd been dying to strut his recovery expertise but knew the moment had to be perfect or Michael wouldn't hear a word of his explanation. Just like Stuart hadn't the first time he heard it.

"Well, by law, you can be held in custody and potentially charged with attempted murder if you have expressed specific intent to commit the crime and have entered the zone of perpetration. In other words, taken steps in the furtherance of the crime."

"You a certified attorney now?" Joanne asks.

"I'm taking night classes."

"Of course, you are. What's next, medical school?"

Heart of Joanne

"I've considered it," Stuart says. Joanne groans and turns away.

"But she hasn't done anything...." Michael says. " . . . hasn't taken any steps other than opening her mouth."

Joanne looks at Michael scratching his chin like an amateur sleuth. A pipe and a deerstalker hat would complete the picture. Stuart raises an eyebrow to Joanne. Just one. Joanne looks out the window at the rain.

"She hasn't done anything, right?" Michael says.

"They put handcuffs on me, Michael! The mother of your child in handcuffs!"

"Jo, what have you done?"

"Jails are rampant with drugs, Michael!"

"She said she purchased the rat poison," Stuart says.

"At Home Depot?" Michael asks Joanne.

"You said it yourself; they sell it over the counter," she says.

"Yeah, I know that but how do you know that?"

"I looked it up on my phone."

"You googled 'rat poison' on your phone?"

"They keep it in the pest section with the roach and ant motels."

"So you just walked into Home Depot and asked where they keep murderous rat poison?"

"We have a rat problem, Michael!"

"We don't have a rat problem!"

"We have a serious rat problem!"

"I've never noticed any rats!"

"That's because you're never home!" Joanne wails and begins to cry. Hard. Sobs. Buckets of tears. A volume that surprises even her. But these tears are real. The tears of a broken heart. The tears of a woman driven to wander the aisles of Home Depot in search of rat poison with the thought of mixing it into a vat of stew and stirring it up like an evil witch and serving it to her husband and watching him cling to his last moments of life, finally noticing her, finally reaching out to her, finally needing her for something other than a sandwich or a late-night fuck.

"She said she hid it in the garage," Stuart says.

"Jesus, Joanne!" Michael says. Joanne tries to sop up her tears with her shirt.

"I didn't want the dog to get into it!"

Michael sits and rubs his face. "What the fuck?" he says. Joanne goes to him and strokes the back of his head.

"Michael," she says, "I lied for you. I lied about what you did to me."

"What did Michael do to you, Joanne?" asks Stuart.

"I didn't do anything to her," Michael barks.

"But you did Michael, and I've kept it a secret."

"Fine, tell everybody. Stuart. The cops. I don't care. I'm a horrible husband and father and man. I clearly suck at all of this or we wouldn't even be here. Tell him. Put me out of my misery because this whole thing is giving me the fucking creeps."

"Joanne," Stuart says, looking at the scratches on Michael's face, then at the bandage on Joanne's forehead. "Did you really fall down a set of stairs?"

Joanne looks Stuart square in the eye. She would never tell the cops or Stuart, not now or under oath, that she got the cut on her head from a windshield or the cut in her mouth from the back of Michael's hand. He'd never done it before and in the darkest recesses of her mind she thought she deserved it. Besides, they would take Madeline, not only from her, but from them both, a ward of the state. Exactly how Joanne had grown up.

She turns to Michael, answering Stuart's question with silence. "Michael . . . I'm going to close my eyes and when I open them, you're going to tell me this whole thing has been a horrible nightmare and we're going to laugh and go home and make love and . . . and Michael, please go out there and tell the police that you believe me." Michael stares at the floor. "Michael?" He doesn't move. "Michael!"

"I don't know!" he says, standing.

"You don't know what?" Joanne says.

"I just don't know."

"You just don't you know *what*?"

"It's just when you hear somebody, your wife, *your wife!* say she's planning to kill you . . . you have to wonder, you know, you gotta wonder where that came from . . . like some kind of thought she's been harboring . . . some kind of dark thought tossing around in her head, and then one day, you know, something's gonna click and outta nowhere she's gonna go off . . . *and do it!* I mean, how do I know? How do I—?"

"Michael, you said you thought about killing me, too."

"Okay, so I thought about if for a split second. But I never planned it . . . never took any steps in that direction . . . maybe once or twice I wished you were dead. It's not like you haven't given me plenty of reasons. And apparently, I've given you some too. But poison is different."

"How's it different?"

"It just seems *different*."

99

"This is insane. This conversation we're having is completely insane."

"Look, Joanne, you didn't just have the thought of *killing* me . . . you had the thought of *poisoning* me. And you bought rat poison! And thought about how you'd get me to eat it! That's different! Poison is different! Nobody's poisoning anymore!"

"Yes, they are!"

"Where?"

"On TV," she says.

"So watching TV made you buy rat poison?"

"It was just off the top of my head."

"Oh, off the top or your head you thought about poisoning me?" Michael says. "What about shooting me?"

"I don't know, Michael, I hate guns."

"Too bad, because they have 'em at Dick's Sporting Goods. You can walk right in and buy those too."

"Good to know," she says.

"You could've stabbed me. What about stabbing me?"

"I can't stand the sight of blood."

"Oh, I see, so you went through all those other options until you got to the trusty, lethal, rat poison job," Michael says.

"I didn't go through all those other *options*," Joanne says, then thinks. "It was just off the top of my head."

"Where maybe you've been storing it for a while!"

Joanne sighs and slides her hands into her pockets like a busted kid. "Truth is, I don't know where it came from."

"I do," Stuart says. Michael and Joanne turn in

unison to Stuart, standing there, back straight, chin out. It's the first thing they've done together in a long time, maybe years. "Sometimes in our subconscious," Stuart continues, "we store unexpressed feelings. Some of a murderous nature, that if denied can proliferate, if ignored begin to fester . . . until they're finally triggered."

"What a load of crap," Joanne says.

"Personally, I think she needs to be evaluated by a mental health professional," Stuart says to Michael.

Joanne can contain herself no longer. She will tear his ugly face from his giant head. Skin him alive! She lunges at Stuart. But Michael grabs her by the waist and spins her around.

"I'm not crazy!" Joanne wails as she tumbles to the floor where Michael leaves her to writhe. "I was making a joke because you ticked me off! You were talking to me in that Nurse Ratched tone and I'm four shitty nights of sleep into withdrawal hell and I didn't appreciate it! So, I made a joke about you and this place and the carbon monoxide guy! I'm sorry!"

"Felix," Stuart says.

"Felix?" Joanne says, breathlessly wiping snot from her nose.

"The carbon monoxide guy's name is Felix."

Joanne stands, wiping tears, straightening her wild hair. "Okay, Felix," she says like an apology. But the dead look in Stuart's eyes says he buys none of Joanne's act and never will.

Joanne turns to Michael, at the window. "Michael, of course Stuart doesn't believe me. Of course, he turned me into the police. That's what he does. He goes around pretending everybody's lying. It makes him feel better for all those years he spent doing the same thing. But Michael, you know me . . . you know I would never do a thing like that."

Michael strokes his beard. He's already wondered what life would look like without Joanne, his wife of ten years. Would he ever find someone to love—or hate—as much as Joanne? Could he raise Madeline alone? Would Joanne last a week on the street? Because that's where, he's convinced, she'll end up without him. On the street where he found her, or maybe downtown by the river where all junkies and hookers and ex-cons go to live *and* die in tattered tents and cardboard boxes.

Michael grabs his coat and walks to the door. "Get your stuff," he says and walks out.

Joanne rushes to the window and holds her breath. When Michael exits the clinic, she exhales. The big cop at the wheel rolls down his window. Michael speaks. They shake hands. Joanne will soon be free to get high and silence the thunder in her head.

She turns to Stuart, defiant. At last. "You think you're pretty smart, don't you?"

"As impossible as it might seem," Stuart says, "I was trying to do both of you a favor."

Joanne grabs her sweater. "By declaring me a sociopath?"

"That may have been uncalled for."

"Uncalled for? I bet you have a few sociopathic tendencies of your own."

"We all do."

"You mean all of *us*."

"Yes, all of us." Stuart reaches to help her with her

sleeve but hesitates. "You know, Joanne, if you think this is going to get any easier, you're wrong. If you think this is someone else's problem, Michael the husband, Stuart the counselor, you're wrong about that too. This is your problem."

Joanne bares her teeth like fangs.

"Well, thank you for those pearls of wisdom," she says, and struts to the door.

"I'm sorry for you," Stuart says. Joanne stops. Stuart knows exactly what button he's pushed.

"*You're . . . sorry . . . for me?*"

Stuart takes a step toward Joanne. "How long before you start using again? The minute you get home? You sneak into the bathroom . . . give yourself a little fix from your secret stash . . . and how long before you start having thoughts . . . *entertaining thoughts* of killing your husband again?"

"I think you've made your point."

"And how long before your daughter Madeline, the curious five-year-old becomes Madeline the damaged twelve-year-old."

"Don't you dare bring my daughter into this!"

"Sneaking into your room . . . "

"Don't you dare!"

"Dousing the insanity you've dumped on her with a hit of your own stuff!"

Joanne reaches for the door. "And Madeline's four not five," she says.

"On the admittance form you said she was five," Stuart says.

"I think I know how old my daughter is."

103

Scott Barry

"I can go get it. It's in my office."

"Michael filled that stupid thing out," Joanne says. "He probably made some stupid fucking mistake."

The door opens and Michael bounds in. Soaked. He had heard their voices down the hall.

"What the hell's going on? I thought we were done here." Michael looks at Joanne. "Let's go." Joanne looks at Stuart. She looks at Michael. She looks at the sweater in her hand.

"Good luck to both of you," Stuart says.

"Let's go." Michael reaches for Joanne's arm. She doesn't move. She can't.

"Michael, how old is Madeline?"

"What?"

"How old is Madeline?" Joanne says.

"How *old* is Madeline?" Michael says.

"How old?"

"Our daughter, Madeline?"

"Michael, tell Stuart how old our daughter Madeline is."

"Joanne, what the—"

"Tell him! I need to hear you say it!" Michael looks at Stuart. He looks at Joanne.

"She's five," he says. "Now let's get outta here."

Joanne turns away so that neither Michael nor Stuart can see her face, not now. Not ever again.

"I need to know how you know that, Michael. I need an example. A *specific* example."

"An example of what?" Michael says.

"Of Madeline being five," Joanne says.

Michael thinks a moment, searching. "Her birthday

this year . . . she had five candles . . . she blew out three . . . then she tried again . . . and blew out the last two. You were right there." Joanne stands frozen and silent. Michael puts her coat over her shoulders. "All right, that's enough. It's been a helluva night. Let's go."

Joanne doesn't move. If ever a living death existed, it lives in her right now.

"Joanne," Michael says, "the cops aren't gonna wait all night, let's go."

"I can't," she says.

"Can't what?"

"Go."

"What do you mean you *can't go?*"

"I have to stay," she says as if those words were spoken *to* her, not *by* her.

"You have to *what*?" Michael says.

"I have to stay," she says, now conscious, now remembering in a tumble of images, why she was in rehab *this* time. This time because of that horrible day, only four days ago when she left Madeline alone in front of the TV and went to her friend Lilly's house to smoke crack and drink vodka. She would go down on Lilly for the crack and trade Michael's codeine for a hit of heroin. She would pass out on Lilly's floor, a drooling mess and awake in a panic, remembering that Madeline was home alone. Lilly would try to stop her, but Joanne would get in her car and drive home. And when she pulled up to their house, she would pause a moment to enjoy those last delicious moments of being high. But when she looked in the rearview mirror to confirm her euphoria, she would gasp at the sight of blood running down her temple. She would scream and notice, as if for the first

105

time, the windshield shattered into a web. She would tumble out of the car on to the asphalt, hysterical, crying and see the front of her car dented. Steam pouring from the radiator. She would see Madeline in the window of their house, crying at the sight of her bloodied mother. She would push away the neighbors trying to help her and stumble into her house. She would call Michael like she always did when she fucked up, and when he arrived, she would order him to call the police and ask if there'd been an accident and if anybody had been hurt, god forbid, a person, a child, on the street, in a crosswalk—she couldn't remember a second of the drive home. The police would say, no, there had been no report of an accident. And Michael would hang up, furious, boiling with rage, and lose himself in a moment of fury and strike Joanne with the back of one of his greasy hands and she would rise from the floor and punch him in the side of the head and claw at his face, his skin and blood lodging under her fingernails. And Michael would call Wellness Recovery in Placerville while Joanne was getting stitches in her forehead at Mercy Hospital in Sacramento. And he would take Madeline to his mother's house and drive Joanne into the foothills where he would fill out her admittance form, and without a word, leave. Leave Joanne to spend the next four days sweating, puking, screaming, until today, when she finally joined Stuart's "sacred circle." Sober. And awake. Threatening to kill her husband.

*

Joanne chews on the loose flesh inside her lip. She touches the bandage on her forehead. These wounds will heal. But what might never heal is the aching truth that no matter how hard she tries she cannot remember her daughter, Madeline, the only reason she has for living, blowing out five candles, any candles, on her fifth birthday.

"I have to stay," Joanne says.

Michael tugs on his beard. "Joanne, after everything we've just been through, you wanna stay? They're not gonna let you stay."

"I have to."

"Will somebody please tell me what the fuck is going on? Stuart?"

"News to me," Stuart says.

"Great, now I'm going crazy," Michael says.

"Michael, you have to trust me," Joanne says.

"*Trust you?*"

"If I walk out that door . . . I can't promise I'll ever come back. I know that sounds crazy . . . but I can't . . . promise. This is it . . . for us. You . . . me . . . Madeline. I have to stay."

Michael strokes her face, her ashen, ghostly face. "Honey, you can't stay. You can't . . . " he looks at Stuart. "Can she?"

Stuart thinks. "I suppose I could make an exception, but only if she agrees to participate—completely."

Joanne looks at Michael. She looks at Stuart. And nods.

"Fine," Michael says, exhausted. "So . . . I guess I'll see you at the end of the month."

"But what about family night next week?" Joanne says. "Madeline's dance recital? I want to hear how it—"

Michael steps back. "She'll be fine. I'll explain . . .

not all of this . . . but enough. It'll give her . . . it'll give us some time."

Michael walks to the door. He wants to turn around and hold Joanne and make it all go away. The lovely Joanne. The love of his life, the only woman he would, could, ever love.

Michael looks at Joanne, then at Stuart, and is gone.

Joanne exhales and walks to the window as Michael arrives at the police cruiser. It's raining harder now. Thunder crackles. Blue lightning flashes in the night sky. Michael nods to the cops, then disappears into the night, the rain, the world out there. He doesn't look back. Joanne knew he wouldn't. She wonders if he'll keep their house for himself and Madeline. Or leave her there alone. She wonders if she'll have to fight to see Madeline. If things will ever be the way she always dreamed they would be; at least the way they were. But she knows that dream—and nightmare—is gone forever. Replaced by another. Just life now. Her life.

She watches the police cruiser pull out, leaving an empty space in the parking lot where the cops had sipped their 7-11 coffee—but at least paid attention to her.

She thinks a moment about Madeline's doll-like face, her porcelain skin, her saucer shaped ocean-blue eyes, her magical giggle, her toothless smile, her silky blonde hair, her skin that smells like the future. She fights off flooding tears. The time for tears has come and gone. The time for Joanne to dig deep into herself—for herself—has arrived.

She glances over her shoulder at Stuart.

PLEASANT THINGS

"You didn't know a damn thing about your grandfather," Senior spoke to Junior as they walked away from St. Joseph's church on that winter day.

The kid, all of twelve, looked up at his dad, shivering.

"You didn't know him," Senior continued. Then he took a drag from his Marlboro Red. "Not the real him."

*

An hour earlier, Junior had stood at the lectern in St. Joseph's and said the kinds of things you're supposed to say about your grandfather who just died. Pleasant things. He talked about his grandfather teaching him to ride a bike down First Street, to roller skate at Skate Country, to swim at the

109

community pool everyone called "The Big Pool". He talked about building sand castles and diving through the waves of the Pacific at Drake's Bay with his grandfather during summer weekends. He talked about riding in the back of his grandfather's '68 Ford truck in the annual Fourth of July parade. He talked about trout fishing and that time they cut down their Christmas tree up in the Sierra Nevada.

But Senior didn't want to hear any of that good-time talk because it was *he* who should've taught Junior those things, taken him to those places—rather than running from himself with booze and drugs and women and missing the kinds of things a father isn't supposed to miss.

And Senior wasn't talking about fathering when he told Junior he didn't know his grandfather. He was talking about something else. Something darker. Junior could tell by the sound of his dad's voice.

But what?

What didn't Junior know about his grandfather? He knew, like the rest of town, that his grandfather was a morning boozer who drove too fast, talked too loudly, and flipped up women's skirts with a brush of his palm against their ass. He even once answered the door naked, flashing his semi-erect dick at a pretty Jehovah's Witness woman who never came back.

These were the stories Junior and his friends retold, sipping Pepsis under the old train bridge in the meadows behind town, laughing wildly. But not Senior. He never laughed when the conversation turned to Junior's grandfather. No, his face turned red, beet red, with sweat on his brow; and he'd light his cigarette in silence and wait for the words to pass.

Pleasant Things

Senior had his gripes with Junior's grandfather and rightly so.

He'd yanked the man out of more bars and sheriff's cruisers than he could count—and his embarrassment had turned to hatred long before the funeral. Everyone in town knew that too. Especially at the funeral, Senior sitting in the back row of the pews, eyes open during every prayer, lips sealed during every reading, heal tapping the floor. "Keep it short," he said to Junior when Junior stood for the lectern.

*

When they arrived at Cousin Stan's house a couple blocks from the church, Senior marched into the kitchen and wrapped one of his calloused hands around a fifth of Early Times whiskey sitting on the counter. A plastic bottle. The cheap stuff. Just how he liked it.

Cousin Stan walked by Senior with a tray of cookies for the other guests. "Figured you'd want that crap," he said to Senior without eye contact.

"Figured right." Senior slid open the kitchen door and walked outside to the wooden porch. He removed the sport coat he'd borrowed from his buddy at the tackle shop, sat in a folding lawn chair and took a swig from the plastic bottle.

Junior sipped hot chocolate from a Styrofoam cup and watched Senior through the sliding glass door. It was too cold outside for Junior. Not Senior. His skin was thick as tire tread and his blood ran so hot he'd hunt ducks in the dead of winter in a T-shirt.

Senior took more swigs. "Get yer own damn

111

whiskey," he hollered to whoever'd listen. "My dad's dead. I'm gonna do whatever the fuck I want today."

Junior left to get another cup of hot chocolate. He knew what came next: Senior waving his arms and shouting in Spanish—exactly what was happening when he returned.

A few cousins had heard the rambling and were gathered round Senior in down jackets. They smoked their cigarettes and laughed at Senior even though they couldn't understand a word he said because his Spanish was bad enough sober, unintelligible when slurred. Even worse he was missing his right front tooth making every "s" sound like "sh."

Senior had torn out the tooth biting into a piece of homemade jerky from a big four-point buck he shot that winter. "Snapped the fucker right off," he had said with a laugh. "That old buck got the best of me yet."

"You gonna get a new tooth, Dad?" Junior had wondered.

"Dunno, kid. Kinda like the way it makes me look. *Mean.*"

*

But Junior could understand every word his dad said when he spoke in Spanish, even through the sliding glass door. Junior's grandmother, Ana, was full-blooded Mexican straight from Guadalajara and spoke *Español* in the house. Junior had a good ear for language too. He'd spent years in speech therapy working on his lisp and his S's.

Junior also knew the story Senior was telling on the porch. Senior had told it many times before, though as far as

Junior knew never to anyone but him. The last time Junior heard the story Senior was planted in his favorite lawn chair in the backyard finishing off a sixer of Coors.

But that was a couple years ago.

Senior was telling it now for all to hear—at the reception for his dead father. Junior closed his eyes tight, wishing his dad would tell a hunting story like he normally did when people were around. But something was on Senior's mind, and he wanted to tell *this* story.

Today.

It went something like this: According to Senior, one night on the way home from work at the local fertilizer plant he stopped to check on his mother, Ana. She was dying of breast cancer. When he arrived at their house his father was passed out in his La-Z-Boy by the fireplace. Ana moaned with sickness from the back bedroom. She'd been on morphine for weeks. But she was coherent enough to tell Senior that Junior's grandfather made her sign a check so he could buy more booze.

Ana's cancer had metastasized and weakened most of her body. She could barely move her hand, let alone stop someone else. Junior's grandfather stuck that pen in her hand and made her sign that check. When Ana finished telling Senior the story, he lost his shit. Said it just like that, "Lost my fucking shit. Set out to kill that motherfucker."

"I drove home like Mario Andretti, grabbed my brand new *nickel-plated* .357 from behind the headboard—don't any of you motherfuckers get any ideas about stealing it—spun that cylinder a couple times to make sure it was set up right, stuck it in the back of my pants and drove back to the house in a downpour where I found that sonofabitch still

113

asleep. Well, I slapped the fucker so hard I knocked out his dentures *and* his old ass clear out of the chair and flat onto his back." Senior laughed and spit to the ground. "I got on my knees and stuck that gun in his mouth, pulled the hammer back and looked him straight in the eye. Was about to pull the trigger and send that sonofabitch to hell when he mumbled, 'Go ahead, kid, pull that fuckin' trigger—if you're man enough.'"

Junior held his breath as Senior paused and looked off into some distance of space and time. Junior knew what came next: "Only reason I let him live," Senior said. Then he took a deep pull on the Early Times and wiped the remnant whiskey from his mouth. "What's the point of killing a man doesn't care if he lives anyhow?"

One of the cousins stamped out his cigarette and shook his head. "Bullshit."

Senior looked at him like he might stick a gun in *his* mouth. Junior downed the last of his hot chocolate and set his cup on the counter. He knew when Senior was telling the truth and when he wasn't. This was one of those times he knew it was the truth. He also knew he might have to run out there and stop Senior from throwing a punch.

Senior held his gaze on his cousin for longer than you'd think. Then he started laughing like a crazy man and tossed the Early Times bottle in the bushes.

"Let's get the hell outta here, kid," he hollered to Junior inside, then struggled to stand and stumbled to the sliding glass door.

*

Junior took the wheel and drove home even though he was only twelve and it was dark out. Senior snored loudly, his head against the window. Junior looked at Senior and swore he'd never become a boozer. If he was going to become addicted to anything, it would be sex. That seemed safest.

*

The next morning Senior knocked on Junior's bedroom door and yelled, "Get yer ass up." Then Senior took two aspirin from the cabinet, grabbed a can of Coors from the fridge and swallowed the pills and the contents of the can in a single chug. Then he belched and laughed.

Junior appeared in the kitchen, rubbing the sleep out of his eyes.

"Gonna clean out the old man's place," Senior said with narrowed eyes. "Put it on the market and sell that fucker." Then he smiled big. "You really wanna know your grandfather . . . come with me."

*

Junior's grandfather's house was a little place a few miles down the levee road from town that he'd built with his own two hands. It had white lap siding, green shutters and a lamp post in the front yard that sat under a big oak tree.

Junior's grandfather was a fine carpenter, everyone agreed, and had built a fine house. That was a long time ago. Now the oak was overgrown, the paint chipped, and inside the place was covered with vodka bottles, soiled clothes, and dirty dishes.

It smelled something awful of human shit.

Junior's grandfather's heart quit on a day like any other, as he climbed out of bed. He tumbled to the floor and the weight of his boozer's belly burst his colostomy bag like a water balloon. The next day Senior hired a couple of Mexican ladies to clean up the mess, but they only got so far before quitting. "Esta casa es muy malo, senor," they said politely, shuffling down the driveway. "No es posible."

Senior couldn't blame them. "Damn hard smell to make go away," he said to Junior now standing in that filthy kitchen. He handed Junior a blue bandana like the red one he wore around his own mouth. Junior tied the bandana tightly around his head. He looked around the kitchen for something, anything, that reminded him of the years he spent living in this house when his dad was gone and his grandparents raised him. He was certain they were the best years of his life. And would always be. Especially when his grandmother was alive. Back then the kitchen smelled of fresh tamales and baked beans. His sheets were clean and his clothes neatly folded. The house was spotless and the patio often filled with the scent of roses from the garden and the sound of Folklorico music from the transistor radio.

"Wait here, kid," Senior said and walked down the hall. Junior looked at the remains of a frozen dinner. The sink piled high with dirty dishes. A cockroach crossed the floor. The house didn't smell like tamales. It smelled like the inside of a garbage can.

"So," hollered Senior from down the hall, "you think you knew your grandfather, huh?"

Junior didn't answer. He stomped on the roach. Then

another. He tightened his bandana.

Senior entered the kitchen, carrying a cardboard box and set it on the table. "Take a look at this." He turned the box upside down and out spilled dozens of old VHS tapes.

Junior looked at the images on the covers: naked women and men devouring each other from all angles. He looked away. Senor chuckled. "Don't be shy, kid, take a good look." Junior looked back, first a peek, then with eyes open wide. Groups. Orgies. Women on women. Men on men. A woman and a donkey. Junior could tell by the floppy ears.

Junior breathed fast breaths, struggling for oxygen.

"Porn, kid," said Senior. "Your grandfather was *addicted* to porn."

Junior squinted at Senior, afraid if he looked too long at the covers he'd get in trouble. Senior lit a Marlboro Red. "Go ahead, kid, see who your grandfather really was." Junior let his eyes rest on one of the covers. A red-haired woman stared at him—and only him—with hungry eyes. He mouthed the title, "Wicked Sensations." He looked at her blood red puckered lips, her round breasts and creamy thighs, her tiny patch of pubic hair. He felt his penis filling inside his jeans. He sat down and hunched over.

"Somethin', huh," Senior said, holding his gaze on Junior for a moment before walking off down the hall again.

*

Junior nearly threw up, but then sat up. He couldn't take his eyes off the red-haired woman. Then he thought about his grandfather—the man who taught him to swim and roller skate and ride a bike—looking at the same woman, watching her. He nearly threw up again. He wondered if his grandfather thought of this kind of thing when they were camping together or catfishing or hunting pheasants. He wondered if it mattered. He wondered if his grandmother knew—or if, god forbid, she had watched these tapes too.

Senior arrived with a new box. "Get a load of this shit," he said, swiping the VHS's to the floor with his forearm before dumping the contents of the new box on the table: magazines. "Biker Chick." "Hustler." "Calientes." Senior opened a magazine to the centerfold. A black woman, legs spread from page to page. Senior dangled her pink vagina in front of Junior's face.

"You really wanna know your grandfather?"

Junior stared at the woman without answering.

"I'm askin' you a question, kid."

"I guess."

"You either do or you don't."

Junior looked away. "Thought I already did."

"You didn't know shit." Senior tossed the magazine into the mess of VHSs on the floor. He produced a manila envelope from the back of his pants and set it on the table. "Go ahead, kid," he said, crossing his arms. "Might as well know. Don't wanna spend your whole life thinking your grandfather was some kind of goddamned saint."

Junior stared at the envelope. He didn't want to open it. He didn't want to know what was inside. But he wanted to know his grandfather. He wanted to know the man who raised him while Senior was running around figuring out what to be when *he* grew up.

"Here," Senior said and bent open the clasp. "Go

ahead."

Junior reached inside and pulled out a stack of black and white photographs. The first one looked like a naked wrestling match, a tangle of arms and legs and tits and ass.

Junior turned it right side up. A naked man and woman were tangled together. Sex. Junior didn't know much, but he knew enough to know what he was looking at.

"Keep goin'," Senior said.

Junior slid the picture off the stack and looked at the next: a self-portrait of a man. Junior looked closer. A self-portrait of his grandfather. Naked. Legs spread, sitting in his La-Z-Boy, facing camera. Semi-erect penis in hand.

Junior swallowed hard and looked at his dad for answers. Senior lifted his bandana, put another Marlboro Red in his mouth, took a drag, and folded his arms. "Your grandfather was also a narcissist."

"A what?" Junior said.

"Somebody who loves looking at their own damn self. Keep goin'."

Junior sighed and reached for the stack. He knew these pictures had been taken with his grandfather's old Rolleiflex camera and developed in the hallway linen closet he'd converted into a darkroom. These photos were his. *All his.* Junior remembered the family photos at holidays and vacations where his grandfather would set the timer on the Rolleiflex and jump into the photo at the last second. He didn't know it was used for other purposes.

Junior thumbed through more pictures of random naked women. Then pictures of women with men. He paused at a picture of a woman with her head between another woman's legs. Something he had heard about from his friends sipping Pepsi under the bridge, but didn't believe. Then a picture of a man and a man, then groups of men. Naked. Together. He'd never heard of this. He pictured his grandfather looking down the Rolleiflex and snapping these pictures. He wondered if his grandfather had jumped into any of them at the last second like he did at Christmas.

"That was him," Senior said. "Your grandfather. He was into *all* of it."

Junior began to cry.

"Keep goin'," Senior said.

Junior shuffled through more photos, wiping tears, stopping at a photo of a naked woman. He focused his eyes. It looked like his grandmother. *It was his grandmother.* His grandmother who had taught him to read, to brush his teeth, who massaged his legs with rubbing alcohol when he had growing pains.

But she wasn't wearing her favorite apron or humming along to a Folklorico song. She was naked, back arched, lying on her side, hand between her legs, mouth open, eyes closed.

She was beautiful . . . and sexy . . . but she was his grandmother.

Junior wiped his eyes. He hated these photos. He hated his grandfather for taking them. He hated his father for showing them to him. He hated his life.

"Better to know the truth," Senior said, putting his hand firmly on his son's shoulder. Junior looked at his father's weathered hand, felt its weight. A hand made of stone.

Junior grabbed the stack of photos and threw them across the room. He ran down the hall into the bathroom and locked the door. He pulled his bandana down to breathe but the bathroom smelled like death. He pulled the bandana back up and began to hyperventilate. *I hate you! I hate you! I hate you! Why can't people be who they're supposed to be! Grandfathers! Grandmothers! Fathers! All of them!*

*

"Nobody has to know any of this," Senior said, dumping the last of the photos into the old incinerator in the backyard. "Just you and me."

Senior grabbed a metal poker and jabbed the fire. Junior watched the thick black smoke of burning plastic rise to the sky.

He tried to remember fishing for trout in the Sierra. He tried to remember riding his bike down First Street. He tried to remember roller skating at Skate Country. He tried to remember diving through the waves at Drake's Bay.

With his grandfather.

Other Books by Happy Living

Snow Valley (2018)
By Jonathan Grant

Finding Your Black Belt (2018)
By Karen Connover

The Greener The Grass (2017)
By Scott Barry

Love Letters from the Grave (2016)
By Paul Gersper

Turning Inspiration into Action (2016)
By Matt Gersper

The Belief Road Map (2016)
By Matt Gersper and Kaileen Elise Sues

Join our community to stay informed of upcoming books, promotions and updates from Happy Living!

We are on a mission to improve the happy of the world, one person at a time.

Our blog is filled with ideas for living with health, abundance, and compassion.

Visit us at www.happyliving.com

Thank You!

Thank you for reading Hunting Everett Redding. If you enjoyed it please leave a review.